SWEET NOW AND FOREVER

A SWEET COVE MYSTERY
BOOK 24

J. A. WHITING

D1528201

To hear about new books and book sales, please sign up for my mailing list at:
jawhiting.com

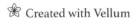 Created with Vellum

With thanks to my readers

Use your magic for good

1

It was a typical morning in Sweet Cove as Angie Roseland headed downstairs to her bakery located in a small part of the Victorian mansion where she and two of her three sisters lived. The aroma of freshly baked scones and cinnamon rolls wafted through the Sweet Dreams Bake Shop as Angie slid a tray of pastries into the display case. She hummed softly to herself, a smile playing over her lips. Early morning was Angie's favorite time of day; she loved how quiet and peaceful it was. The bakery with its cream-colored walls, crystal chandelier, exposed brick accent wall, and cozy fireplace always felt so full of promise at the start of a new day.

Angie made her way around the shop, stopping to straighten a framed photo on the mantel and fluff a pillow on the overstuffed chairs near the front windows. Her motions were slow and deliberate as she infused each task with positive emotions. She had a special skill as a baker where she could put intention into the things she made, optimism, joy, warmth — and the person who ate the item would experience those feelings. It was a ritual of sorts for Angie, a way to spread good vibes to everyone who entered the bake shop's doors.

When the former owner of the Victorian mansion, Professor Marion Linden, passed away, she left the home and property to Angie, along with her beloved orange Maine Coon cat, Euclid. Now, Euclid and another cat, Circe, were members of the Roseland family. In addition to the Victorian, there was a large two-story carriage house that stood behind the house. The first floor consisted of a two-car garage and a storage section, but the second floor had two apartments, each with a kitchen-living room area, bathroom, and two bedrooms.

Satisfied with her preparations, Angie unlocked the front door and flipped the closed sign to open. She drew in a deep breath, embracing the warm, late summer air. Her two employees arrived within minutes and hurried to start the morning tasks, and in thirty minutes, the first customers of the day would flock inside.

As she opened some of the windows to let in the fresh air, Angie spotted a familiar face shuffling down the sidewalk. Pete Thompson lived just around the corner and frequented the bake shop nearly every morning for his daily scone and coffee. The elderly man gave a little wave as he cracked open the front door.

"Morning, Pete," Angie called out cheerfully. "The usual today?"

"You bet." Pete chuckled. "Can't start my day without one of your blueberry scones."

Angie packaged up the scone and poured a steaming cup of coffee while Pete settled into his favorite armchair. More customers began to trickle in - Shirley with her two poodles, bike messenger Sam on his way to work, and mothers with strollers meeting for gossip over lattes. Angie greeted each one by name, exchanging a few friendly words as she handed them their orders. She loved the predictable small town rhythm.

By afternoon, the bakery hummed with its usual comforting activity of serving tourists and townsfolk. Outside on the porch, patrons sat chatting at the bistro tables or stared out at the sunny street. Inside, people laughed and mingled among the mismatched chairs and sofas. Angie and her staff kept busy, replenishing displays and offering refills of coffee.

She paused to gaze out at the street as people strolled past heading down to the beach. She loved the life she'd built in Sweet Cove. Her sisters lived close by, her husband Josh was just a phone call away at the resort he owned, and their little daughter Gigi would be waking soon from her nap. Angie smiled thinking about her sweet, affectionate child with Josh's soft hair and her own inquisitive blue eyes.

The tinkle of the shop door opening pulled Angie from her thoughts. She glanced up expecting to see another customer's familiar face but instead met the bright, smiling eyes of her sister Jenna.

"Hey, you," Angie called, coming around the counter to embrace her twin in a hug. The two sisters shared an unmistakable bond.

Jenna and Angie were fraternal twins who didn't share many physical characteristics. Angie was the oldest by a few minutes and looked more like Court-ney, and Jenna was taller than her twin and had long, dark brown hair, but all the sisters shared the same big, blue eyes they'd inherited from their mother.

"I just dropped Libby off with Mr. Finch for a few hours," Jenna explained, keeping her voice low. "I thought I'd come help you close up."

Angie checked her watch, surprised to see it was already late in the afternoon. "That would be great, thanks. I don't know where the day went. Today flew by."

The twins worked in easy sync, clearing dishes, wiping down tables, and packaging up leftover baked goods. As they swept the porch, Jenna gave Angie a knowing glance.

"So, only three more weeks until the big event," she said with a playful nudge. "How's our bride-to-be holding up?"

Angie laughed. "Oh, you know Courtney, she's laid-back, organized, and ready. Between her and Ellie, I think they have every minute scheduled for the wedding and reception."

Courtney's wedding to her British lawyer boyfriend, Rufus Fudge, was slated to be a small, intimate affair. The ceremony would take place right in the Victorian's lovely backyard garden, followed by dinner and dancing on the beautiful yacht Josh had purchased to use for resort events.

Jenna nodded, leaning on her broom. "Ellie's almost finished with Courtney's gown, and then she'll schedule fittings for our bridesmaid dresses. I'm so happy for Courtney and Rufus."

"Me, too." Angie smiled. "If ever a couple was meant to be, it's them. Remember when they first met outside the candy store? Electricity flashed between them like nothing I've ever seen."

"Yeah." Jenna chuckled. "Their eyes were like heat-seeking missiles locked on each other."

A comfortable silence settled between the sisters as they continued tidying up.

Jenna cleared her throat softly, breaking the quiet. "So, something kind of weird happened on my way over here."

Angie paused her sweeping, detecting an odd note in Jenna's voice. "What is it? Is everything okay?"

"Yeah, of course," Jenna said quickly ... too quickly.

Angie noticed her fiddling with the beaded bracelets crowding her slender wrist. She fixed her sister with a probing stare. "What's up? I can tell something's bothering you."

Jenna let out a reluctant sigh, her shoulders

slumping. Angie knew her twin could never keep anything from her for long.

"It's probably nothing. I just saw a strange car outside the Victorian earlier. It gave me a weird vibe."

Angie tensed. Their family had endured more than their fair share of trouble over the years. She knew not to ignore even a hint of potential worry.

"Tell me exactly what you saw," she prompted gently.

"Libby and I were walking up Beach Street from home," Jenna began. "There was a car parked across from the Victorian, a dark color, maybe blue or black. I couldn't really make out the driver because of the glare on the windows."

She met Angie's concerned gaze. "But as soon as they noticed us coming, they took off - just sped away, tires screeching."

Angie frowned. Something in Jenna's voice gave her pause. She knew her highly intuitive sister couldn't be dismissed.

"Could you tell what kind of car it was?" Angie asked.

Jenna shook her head apologetically. "Some kind of SUV. It had those dark tinted windows. It happened so fast, I didn't get a good look at it."

Angie considered this, absently running her fingers over the tulip carved into the porch railing. She stared off down the sun-bathed street, suddenly wary.

Sweet Cove was an idyllic place, but they weren't immune to nuisance or crime.

Could the car and its occupant be a warning sign of something more sinister on the horizon? Angie gave herself a little shake, not wanting her thoughts to spiral down that path. She wanted to think it was just a random passerby who took a wrong turn, but she knew better than that.

She turned back to Jenna with a reassuring smile. "I'm sure it will be okay, but we should be aware and tell the others what you experienced."

Jenna managed a weak smile in return. "Yeah, you're right. We'll be okay, whatever this might become."

Angie gave her sister a quick hug. "Come on, let's go to your studio. I promised to help you pack up those online orders."

Jenna nodded, following her sister into the bakery to gather their things, but Angie could see her twin's shoulders remained tense, and her smile was tinged with a bit of unease.

Try as she might, Angie couldn't fully shake her

own small, creeping dread as she locked the bake shop door. For all her focus on infusing her pastries with positive vibes each morning, shadows still found a way to intrude.

As Angie and Jenna made their way into the kitchen of the Victorian, Angie glanced over her shoulder for just a moment to look out at the street, half expecting to glimpse a strange, dark car parked there.

But the road was empty and quiet in the soft afternoon light.

2

Jenna and Angie entered through the door into the spacious farmhouse-style kitchen with its high-end cabinets, wood floors, and granite countertops. At the sound of the door opening, two cats came padding into the room, their tails held high.

"There you are," Angie cooed, bending to stroke each of the cats. Euclid, the huge Maine Coon, nudged his orange and white head against her hand, while the petite black cat Circe wove figure eights around Angie's ankles.

Jenna chuckled. "I think they missed us."

"Want to come into the studio with us?" Angie asked the cats. Two pairs of unblinking eyes stared back at her, and Circe let out a meow. Angie took that as a yes.

The four of them made their way through the kitchen and down the long hall lined with family photos, to the back corner of the house. Jenna's jewelry studio occupied a large open room that had once been a library. Display cases of glittering necklaces and racks of beaded handbags lined the walls. A worktable strewn with pliers, spools of wire, and trays of beads dominated one side of the room.

"I'm looking forward to seeing how your new fall jewelry line is coming along," Angie told her twin as she settled onto a cream-colored leather sofa along the back wall, with Euclid and Circe jumping up beside her. Late afternoon sun filtered in through the tall windows, lending a warm glow to the cozy creative space.

Jenna immediately got to work cleaning up her crowded worktable. "Sorry for the mess," she said a bit sheepishly. "I've been struggling to get this new collection finished."

Angie stood to survey the autumn-hued beads, delicate chains, and metal charms scattered across the tabletop. She imagined how they would come together into Jenna's signature earthy-style jewelry.

"This all looks amazing," Angie offered sincerely. She knew her sister was sometimes prone to self-doubt when it came to starting a new line of her designs.

Jenna managed a small, grateful smile in return. She held up a few pieces she had completed - a necklace with a copper oak leaf pendant, bronze feather earrings, and a bracelet threaded with crimson glass beads.

"I feel like something is still missing though," Jenna confessed with a frustrated sigh. She sank onto her work stool, her chin resting in her hands.

Angie examined the jewelry spread before her, picturing the way the pieces would look layered together. The warm metallics and pops of crimson made her think of cozy autumn strolls and lush fall foliage. But Jenna was right - the collection still needed a little something more.

Angie's gaze landed on a twisted branch of real oak leaves Jenna kept on her supply shelf. "What if you added in some real pieces of preserved leaves or flower petals?" she suggested. "I think blending in natural elements would make the line really special."

Jenna's eyes lit up at the suggestion. "I really like that idea. I can't believe I didn't think of it." She sprang up from her stool and pulled Angie into an impulsive hug. "Thank you. This collection is going to be amazing now."

Angie laughed, returning the enthusiastic embrace. She loved seeing her sister bubble over with creative excitement.

The two chatted as Angie packaged up some online jewelry orders while her sister drew ideas on her sketch pad and then assembled more pieces incorporating golden and russet beads. Angie admired Jenna's skillful wire-wrapping and delicate soldering work as she carefully packed each order into a branded gift box.

After an hour or so, Jenna set down her soldering iron with a satisfied sigh. "I think that's enough for today. My hands are starting to cramp." She flexed her slender fingers.

Angie placed one last order into its shipping envelope. "It's going to be stunning when it's all finished."

Jenna gave her sister a smile. She leaned back against the work table, gazing thoughtfully at her array of assembled jewelry. Angie sat down on the sofa and settled against the cushions, idly stroking Euclid's thick fur as he purred contentedly.

Abruptly, Jenna stiffened, her eyes widening.

Angie straightened, instantly on alert. "What's wrong?"

Jenna held up a hand, staring fixedly just beyond

Angie's left shoulder. The blood had drained from her face.

Alarmed, Angie swiveled around, seeing nothing but the blank sunlit wall. She turned back to her sister.

"Jenna, you're freaking me out. What is it?"

Jenna gave herself a little shake, dragging her gaze to meet Angie's. "Sorry, I just ... I saw something."

Angie tensed. Her sister occasionally saw things invisible to the rest of them - ghosts, visions, omens. Jenna's sixth sense could be a blessing or a curse. Right now, Angie feared it was signaling the latter.

"What did you see?" she prodded gently.

Jenna hesitated, looking uneasy. She toyed with a tangle of wire coils, avoiding Angie's probing stare. Finally ,she spoke, her voice barely above a whisper. "It was a ghost. A woman. Standing over there." She gestured vaguely over Angie's shoulder. "She was staring right at me. I haven't seen a ghost for a while. She startled me."

A chill went through Angie that had nothing to do with the room's temperature. "Was she familiar to you? What did she look like?"

Jenna frowned and shook her head, thinking about the image in her mind's eye. "I don't know who she is. She's young, maybe in her late twenties. She had on a flowy printed dress. Her eyes were a brilliant shade of blue and her hair was dark blonde and kind of messed, like she'd been out in the wind. She looked ... agitated."

As her heart raced, Angie waited silently for her sister to continue.

"Her mouth was moving like she wanted to tell me something." Jenna dropped her gaze to her hands again.

"What was she saying?" Angie prodded gently.

Jenna lifted her eyes reluctantly, full of unease. "She said ... danger is coming ... coming for the family."

Icy anxiety flooded Angie's veins as every protective instinct flared inside her. She thought back to Jenna's encounter with the mysterious car earlier that day and her own lingering unease. This specter's warning could not be ignored.

Jenna looked at her sister apprehensively, clearly unsettled by Angie's tense reaction. "I'm probably just tired. I probably misinterpreted her message," she backpedaled unconvincingly.

Euclid let out a hiss.

Angie crossed the room and took her sister's hands in hers, gazing into her uncertain face. "This isn't because you're tired and overworked. You never misinterpret a ghost's communication." She gave Jenna's hands a reassuring squeeze. "We're going to figure this out. We won't let anything happen to the family."

Jenna managed a tiny smile, comforted by her twin's certainty.

"Let's go talk to Mr. Finch," Angie suggested. "We need to tell him about the car and this ghost's message, and we should probably tell Chief Martin, too."

As the sisters left the studio with the cats, switching off lights and heading to Mr. Finch's apartment off the family room, Angie couldn't prevent a cold whisper of dread from sliding down her spine. They would keep the family safe, no matter what.

But what menacing forces were converging on their little seaside town of Sweet Cove?

Angie, Jenna, and the cats headed to the first-floor family room of the Victorian to talk to Mr. Finch. Angie knew if anyone could provide insight into Jenna's ghostly encounter, it was their dear family friend.

Mr. Finch was standing next to the open door to his suite of rooms tucked away in the back corner of the house. Fresh flowers adorned the coffee table, and framed artwork lined the living room walls. The smell of simmering tomato sauce wafted from the kitchen.

Despite his age, the white-haired gentleman was fit and trim but walked with a cane due to an injury he suffered decades ago. Mr. Finch's wise blue eyes crinkled at the corners when he saw the sisters. He had long considered the Roseland sisters the grand-daughters he'd never had.

"I've been waiting for you. I knew you were coming. I've been feeling uneasy all day. I sense trouble is brewing, but I don't know what sort it is. Come into the kitchen. I'll make tea and we can talk."

Peering past him, Angie spotted two small figures clustered around the table in the sunroom, crayons clutched in chubby fists. Her almost four-year-old daughter Gigi looked up and broke into a wide grin that perfectly mirrored Angie's.

"Mommy!" she cried, running to the kitchen and launching herself into Angie's arms. Angie scooped her up, kissing the top of her sweet head. Gigi's cousin Libby hurried into the room to hug Jenna.

Angie raised an eyebrow at Mr. Finch. "I hope they haven't been too much trouble for you."

He waved a hand dismissively. "These angels? Never. We've had a delightful afternoon drawing and reading stories, haven't we, girls?"

Gigi nodded enthusiastically. "I made you a picture for the fridge, Mommy."

"Can't wait to see it, sweet pea." Angie set her down with one last smooch. "Why don't you and Libby keep coloring? Aunt Jenna and I need to talk to Mr. Finch about boring grown-up stuff."

The two little girls scurried back to their art projects as Mr. Finch bustled about the kitchen making tea. The scent of the fresh tomato sauce reminded Angie they needed to figure out dinner, but first, they needed Mr. Finch's counsel.

As Jenna relayed the odd events of the day over steaming mugs of tea, Angie watched Mr. Finch's brow furrow deeper and deeper. He tapped his spoon thoughtfully against the rim of his cup once the young woman had finished her tale.

"I must admit, I've sensed a sort of ... heaviness in the air. I've been expecting a call from Phillip with troubling news, but so far, there hasn't been a word from him." Chief Phillip Martin was a friend of the family and knew about their paranormal abilities. He often called them in to help on difficult cases.

Angie bit her lip. She respected Mr. Finch's intuition far more than she trusted her own. If he sensed imminent danger, she was certain it was something serious.

"What do you make of Jenna seeing the ghost?" she asked anxiously.

Mr. Finch took a long sip of tea, contemplating before lifting his eyes to Jenna. "Your gift is always accurate. If you say a spirit cautioned you, we would be foolish not to heed the warning."

He studied the young woman over the rim of his glasses. "I think you should tell me more about the encounter. Try to recall the precise words and feelings."

Angie nodded. "I agree."

Euclid and Circe sat near the table listening to the conversation.

As Jenna haltingly relayed every detail surrounding the spirit woman and her cryptic warning, Mr. Finch listened intently, frowning into his mug. When Jenna had finished, he drummed his fingers on the table, his face creased in thought.

"I felt this ghost was trying to protect us," Jenna clarified.

Mr. Finch exhaled heavily. "Then I am inclined to trust the message. We must be vigilant. You also spotted a suspicious vehicle earlier?"

As Jenna recounted the incident with the dark SUV, Angie felt her anxiety winding tighter. Danger seemed to press in on them from all sides, yet its shape remained hidden. She felt powerless from the unseen threat.

Sensing her rising unease, Mr. Finch reached over to pat her hand reassuringly. "All will be well, my dear. Forewarned is forearmed. We will watch and wait."

Just then Gigi and Libby came careening into the kitchen waving their artwork. "Look what we made!"

Angie summoned up a smile. "These are so beautiful. Let's put them right on Mr. Finch's refrigerator."

As the girls did a little happy dance, Angie peered out the window. She could see her younger sister, Ellie, outside snipping dead blooms from the rose garden she had nurtured for years.

"Hey, I see Aunt Ellie," Angie said brightly. "Who wants to help her with flowers? I think the fresh air will do us all some good."

Angie and Jenna herded the girls outside into the late afternoon sunlight, with the cats and Mr. Finch leading the way. Angie drew in a deep breath, willing her whirling thoughts to slow, but dread still churned in her veins despite the pretty scene in the garden.

Ellie stood up from the flower bed, brushing dirt from her knees. "Hey there, it's a beautiful afternoon."

Angie managed a tense smile. Part of her wished the unknown trouble would just arrive rather than loom over them. It would be better to confront the danger head-on than have to put up with the agonizing wait.

3

They made their way to the sprawling gardens behind the Victorian home, welcoming the fresh air after the dark conversation indoors.

Ellie loved planting and tending the gardens, and they'd flourished under her care. She pushed back the wide-brimmed straw hat shielding her face from the sun and looked at her sisters and Mr. Finch with a curious expression.

"What's going on? You look so serious," she remarked. "Is something wrong?"

Angie sighed, gazing out at the beautiful grounds her sister had nurtured. Flower beds bursting with vibrant blossoms surrounded an open lawn with a stone fire pit to one side. Wisteria climbed the wooden pergola providing shade where the family and B & B guests often gathered for outdoor meals. Usually, this space relaxed Angie, but today it did little to ease her worries.

She turned to Ellie. "It's been a strange day. Let's sit and we'll catch you up."

The foursome settled into the cushioned chairs beneath the pergola's draping vines. Mr. Finch lowered himself gingerly, his cane resting against the side table, and the two cats, Euclid and Circe, curled up in a patch of sunlight near his feet.

Haltingly, Jenna and Angie took turns filling in Ellie on the odd events - the dark SUV speeding away from the house, Jenna's vision of the ghostly warning, and Mr. Finch's own unease. Ellie's blue eyes widened as she listened.

"Oh, gosh," she murmured once they had finished. "It's no wonder you all look so shaken. I was hoping we could enjoy the weeks leading up to the wedding, but this is serious stuff."

"My thoughts exactly, Miss Ellie," Mr. Finch said gravely. "Something troubling is heading our way, I'm afraid."

Before they could discuss any more, the back door swung open, and the youngest Roseland sister came bouncing out, her honey blonde hair glinting in the sun.

"Hey, what's cookin'?" Courtney asked brightly, though her smile disappeared when she saw their tense expressions.

Angie gestured for her sister to join them under the pergola. "We were just telling Ellie about some strange happenings today. I think you should hear this, too."

As Angie recapped the vehicle and supernatural warning, Courtney's eyes grew wide with worry. "Well, our peace and quiet are about to disappear," she said when her sister had finished.

Jenna nodded gravely. "I know. My intuition is telling me we can't ignore the incidents."

Courtney bit her lip, looking uneasy. "Well, if we're sharing weird occurrences, I might as well tell you about this." She pulled a small envelope from her pocket. "I found this on the counter at the candy shop when I opened up this morning."

She withdrew a card with her name written in elaborate cursive on the front. Inside was a short poem and a charm bracelet with beads spelling out her name.

"The note just said it was from a secret admirer," Courtney told them with a small shrug.

Angie frowned, examining the bracelet and lines

of the poem. "Do you have any idea who it could be from?"

"No clue." Courtney sighed. "At first I thought it was sweet, but the more I look at it, the more it gives me the creeps." She absently twisted the diamond ring Rufus had given her when they became engaged.

"It's probably just a harmless crush, but with everything else going on..." Angie's voice trailed off uncertainly.

Before they could say any more, the gate to the garden creaked open and the family looked up to see Rufus striding toward them, his ginger hair flaming in the sunlight. Though a lawyer by trade, he had a casual, artistic style.

Courtney's face broke into a smile when she saw her fiancé. She jumped up to greet him as he swept her into a tight embrace.

"Did I miss anything exciting?" Rufus asked, keeping an arm wrapped around Courtney as they took seats with the others.

Mr. Finch quickly updated Rufus on the strange doings as Courtney showed him the note from the secret admirer. Rufus studied the bracelet, his handsome face creasing into a frown.

"Have you received anything like this before?" he asked Courtney, who shook her head.

"Hopefully it's just an isolated incident then," Rufus said, though he sounded uneasy. Holding Courtney's hand, his fingers brushed over the diamond ring on her finger, and a tiny flame briefly flared around his thumb - a sign of emotion for the fiery empath. Rufus, who had moved to the United States several years ago to work as a lawyer at Jack's firm, had recently discovered that he had a special skill. The men in the family had been working with Mr. Finch to see if they could uncover some "special" skills, and to everyone's surprise, Rufus developed a fire skill. By pointing or gesturing at something, he was able to set it on fire. He would practice by lighting the fire pit or some candles, and almost a year ago, he helped save Ellie from a killer by employing his fire ability.

Angie knew Rufus' presence had a calming influence on their family. She hoped his level head might help make sense of the odd events, but before they could return to the topic, Jenna suddenly stood up staring with wide eyes across the lawn at her daughter Libby, who stood alone near the gardens gazing off into the distance. She hurried over to the little girl.

"Libby, what are you looking at?" she asked the child gently.

"That lady over there," Libby said, pointing toward the empty yard. "The one in the blue dress."

Jenna's face paled. She turned quickly, seeing nothing but grass and trees swaying in the breeze.

She knelt down before her daughter. "What lady, sweetie?"

"The ghost lady," Libby replied matter-of-factly. The little girl had inherited her mother's ability to sense and see ghosts, and because it was normal to her, she'd taken it all in stride. "The ghost lady wants me to give Courtney and Rufus a message."

Jenna went still. Dread crept down Angie's spine as she exchanged an alarmed look with Mr. Finch.

With effort, Jenna kept her voice calm. "What message, Libby?"

The child furrowed her brow as if trying to recall the precise words. "She said ... Courtney and Rufus shouldn't be together. She said it two times." The little girl held up two of her tiny fingers.

Both cats flicked their tails, and Euclid arched his back and hissed.

Gasps rang out across the yard as Courtney's face turned white as a sheet. She gripped Rufus' hand so tightly her knuckles blanched.

"Wh-what?" Courtney stammered, looking faint. "Why would she say that?"

Rufus wrapped an arm around her, distress etched on his face.

Mr. Finch stood abruptly. "Let's go inside. We must discuss this further."

As they filed into the living room, Courtney clung to Rufus, her usual bubbly demeanor extinguished. She looked small and fragile, and Rufus kept an arm securely around her, his jaw set in a hard line.

Angie's thoughts raced. Two spectral warnings in one day, both pointing to imminent, unknowable danger. She met Mr. Finch's grim expression and knew he shared her dread.

Whatever dark forces were aligning against them, Angie feared this was only the beginning.

As everyone headed to the family room, Ellie went to the kitchen for cookies and two pitchers of iced tea and lemonade and quickly returned to join the others. She set the cookie platter on the table and poured a drink for those who wanted one.

Mr. Finch nodded at Jenna, and the young woman turned to her daughter.

"Honey, can you tell us more about the ghost in the yard? What did she look like?"

Libby nibbled on a cookie. "She had yellow hair."

"Was she tall or short?"

"She was regular."

"You said she was wearing a blue dress?"

Libby nodded and took another bite of her cookie. "It was pretty. It moved in the breeze." She moved her hand around like it was floating.

"Can you tell me anything else about how she looked?"

After thinking for a few seconds, Libby said, "She seemed nice."

Gigi was on the floor playing with her toy horses. "She wants to keep us safe."

Everyone looked at the blonde-haired youngster.

"How do you know that?" Angie asked.

Gigi didn't look up. "I can just tell."

"Did she talk to you?"

"Not really."

"Could you see her?"

"No, only Libby can see her. But I can feel her."

"Do you feel anything else from her?" Angie questioned.

With a shrug, Gigi said, "I don't know."

Angie and Jenna exchanged puzzled looks.

"Why doesn't she want me and Rufus to be

together?" Courtney's voice trembled as she posed the question to the little girls.

"She tried to tell me more, but her voice was soft. I can't hear everything she says. It's like the TV when the sound is turned up and down. Can me and Gigi play on the porch?"

"Yeah, sure," Jenna said distractedly, then she sat up thinking of the car that was parked outside earlier. "Wait. Maybe not on the porch. You can play in the yard if Euclid and Circe go with you. I'll come out in a few minutes."

The kids picked up their toys and followed the cats out to the backyard.

"Does Libby's description of the ghost match the spirit you encountered in your studio today?" Angie questioned.

"It's hard to say since Libby didn't give me a lot to go on." Jenna sighed. "But she did mention yellow hair. The ghost I saw had blonde hair so there's a very good chance they're one and the same."

"What the heck is going on?" Courtney seemed close to tears.

Rufus stood and began to pace around the room. "If that ghost thinks she's going to frighten me into not marrying Courtney, she's got another thing coming." Tiny sparks flickered from the ends of the young man's fingers.

Ellie said, "Rufus, your fingers. Don't burn the house down. There's enough going on right now."

"Oh, sorry." Rufus rubbed his hands together and the flickering stopped.

"Does my secret admirer have something to do with all of this?" Courtney ran a hand over her face.

"It's possible," Mr. Finch admitted. "Tell us again how you found the envelope."

After taking a deep breath, Courtney said, "It was on the counter this morning when I opened the candy shop. Madison closed up last night. She left a note with the envelope saying someone left it for me."

"Maybe she got a look at the person," Jenna suggested.

Courtney reached for her phone and texted the young woman. In a few minutes, Madison replied. *I didn't see who left it. I went to the backroom to get some more candies to fill the shelves and when I came back out front, the envelope was on the counter.*

"Do you think the security cameras caught the person on video?" Ellie asked.

Courtney looked hopeful. "Maybe. It's pointing more at the door, but it must have captured his image as he was coming in and leaving. I'll check when I go there tonight."

"Excellent," Mr. Finch told the young woman, and a few seconds later, he asked, "May I hold the bracelet he left for you?"

Courtney nodded and removed the beaded bracelet from her pocket as if she wanted to throw it away like a piece of trash. She walked over to where Mr. Finch was sitting on the sofa and sat next to him. "Here. See what you can sense." She placed it in his hand.

Closing his eyes, Mr. Finch felt the familiar buzz of electricity in his palm as he held the object. A minute later, his eyes opened. "I feel many complicated emotions coming from the bracelet ... admiration, attraction, jealousy, anger. I believe you might be familiar with the person who left this for you. I can't tell if the energy is male or female. This won't be a one-time thing."

Courtney's heart dropped. "Should we tell Chief Martin?"

"I believe that would be the smart thing to do," Mr. Finch replied. "Perhaps he could meet us at the candy shop later today when we go to check on the security videos."

"Will you text the chief, Angie?" Courtney rested

her head against the sofa back. "I can't even think straight."

"I'll do it right now." Angie shook her head at how quickly worry and fear could show up. This certainly wasn't the way she thought the day would go when she woke up that morning.

4

Angie, Jenna, Courtney, Rufus, and Mr. Finch, along with the two cats, made their way to the candy shop on Main Street, hoping to find clues about Courtney's secret admirer in the security footage. When she opened the door, the chimes above it jingled merrily despite the somber mood of the search party.

Inside, the cozy shop was filled with colorful rows of sweets - jars of gumdrops, licorice ropes, chocolates, and more. The shelves and accent walls were painted in cheery pastels. Courtney and Rufus met for the first time outside the shop on opening day several years ago, and the minute they laid eyes on one another, they were smitten. Usually, Courtney loved being surrounded by the sights and scents of their candy business, but today, the charming interior did little to lift her spirits.

They greeted the employees, and then Courtney led the group past the counter to the small office space in the back, with the cats trotting along behind them. Angie gave Courtney's arm a supportive squeeze before her sister switched on the computer monitor displaying grainy security camera footage.

They gathered around as Courtney scrolled through the recording from the previous evening, fast-forwarding on the screen to just about closing time.

"There. That person put the envelope on the counter." Angie pointed. "Rewind the video a bit to see him enter the shop."

Courtney touched the button to make the video go back a few seconds until the person appeared entering the shop, his face obscured by a baseball cap and wearing a big baggy jacket. His hair was either short or tucked up under the cap. The person hurriedly moved around the other customers and placed an envelope on the counter while the clerk was out of the frame, and then he rushed back out the door.

"Can you zoom in?" Rufus asked, leaning closer.

Courtney enlarged the image, but the result was

disappointingly unclear, the features blurred beyond recognition. A few other customers milled about, partially blocking the view.

She sighed heavily, closing the footage. "It's useless. We can't even tell if it's a man or a woman."

The others exchanged discouraged looks and Angie shook her head. "I was sure the video would give us something to go on. Now what?"

As if in reply, the shop's bells jingled again, and a few moments later, Chief Phillip Martin's familiar sturdy frame filled the doorway of the office. The family quickly caught him up on the unsettling recent events. He listened while they took turns telling him about the car parked in front of the Victorian, the two ghosts, their messages that danger was coming, that Courtney and Rufus shouldn't be together, and the secret admirer leaving a note and a handmade bracelet for Courtney.

"You all have every right to be concerned," Chief Martin agreed once they had finished. "In fact, I was just about to give you a call."

A scurry of anxiety pulsed along Angie's skin.

The chief went on to tell them about a young woman in the nearby town of Silver Cove. She had been stalked and harassed by an unknown admirer for about three weeks prior to her wedding. Tragically, she was killed in her home the night before the ceremony was to take place.

As the blood drained out of her face, Courtney inhaled sharply and gripped Rufus' hand. "Oh my gosh! Do you think the killer could be the person who left the note and bracelet for me?"

The chief held up a hand. "In light of the similarities, I'm assigning a patrol car to drive past the Victorian and the candy shop every so often. I'd love to assign an officer to stay with you 24-7, but we just don't have the budget for that."

Rufus' jaw tightened. "Doesn't sound like nearly enough if some lunatic is running loose out there targeting my fiancée."

"We're exploring all angles," Chief Martin assured him calmly. "In the meantime, everyone should take extra precautions - don't go anywhere alone, be aware of your surroundings, keep your doors locked, and notify me immediately if you notice anything suspicious."

Mr. Finch, who had been quietly thoughtful during the discussion, finally spoke up. "As I say, forewarned is forearmed. We must remain vigilant, but not allow fear to overtake us. We need to be able to think straight and clear and keep our wits about us so we can sense danger before it strikes. Woe to the person who targets this family."

The others murmured in agreement, but the atmosphere remained tense.

Courtney spoke with a shaky voice. "How was the young woman in Silver Cove killed?"

The chief hesitated for a few beats, then said, "She was killed with a knife. I'd like you to carry pepper spray with you at all times. If some of you feel up to it, I'd like to take you to the crime scene ... see if you can sense anything there."

Angie, Courtney, Rufus, and Mr. Finch agreed to meet the chief in Silver Cove tomorrow. After fifteen minutes of further discussion, Chief Martin left to return to the station.

Angie turned to Courtney and Rufus. "Rufus, why don't you stay with us at the house if you'd like? At least until we have some answers."

Courtney opened her mouth to protest but Rufus cut her off. "I think that's an excellent idea."

"We'll feel better having you close," Angie told him.

Courtney relented with a weak smile. "Okay, I know when I'm outnumbered. A pajama party it is." But her smile didn't reach her worried eyes.

On the walk back to the house from the candy

shop, the group remained uncharacteristically quiet, each lost in their own anxious thoughts. The two cats seemed especially vigilant as they made their way down Main Street to Beach Street.

Angie's mind spun like the breeze gusting around them. It seemed impossible that only that morning her greatest concern had been perfecting a new scone recipe. Now their safe and peaceful lives felt threatened by something unknown.

When they returned to the Victorian, Ellie was standing on the porch to meet them, her face lined with concern. "How did it go? What did you learn?"

They told her the news as they moved inside to the kitchen, where Euclid and Circe jumped up to the top of the refrigerator. Mr. Finch put tea on, listening as the others discussed the next steps.

"We need to bring Tom, Jack, and Josh into the loop," Jenna told them.

Angie glanced up at the cats. "The men need to know what's going on. We can explain everything before dinner tonight."

The others agreed as Mr. Finch distributed steaming mugs. For a few moments, the only sounds were the clinking of spoons and sipping of tea.

"I hate feeling like we're under attack from some creep and we can't even see his face," Rufus finally said through gritted teeth as his fingers sparked.

Mr. Finch gave him a concerned look. "Remember to mind your emotions, Rufus. Anger will cloud your judgment and interfere with your abilities. We will all need clear heads to keep one another safe."

Rufus took a deep breath until the flickering sparks coming from his fingertips stopped flashing. "You're right. I understand. It just chafes to sit here waiting for this psycho's next move."

"Unfortunately, patience and vigilance are our only weapons right now," Mr. Finch said sagely, though his own wrinkled face was full of concern.

Angie met Courtney's frightened gaze, wishing she could ease her sister's mind, but the truth was, they were all shaken by the looming sense of menace.

They had faced danger before as a family and Angie knew this time their skills would be tested like never before, but she repeated in her mind Mr. Finch's words like a mantra ... forewarned is forearmed.

After they finished their tea, Jenna decided to take Libby home for a while and then return for dinner. "We'll keep things light for the girls tonight.

There's no need to frighten them with all of this ... although they've always been pretty resilient in the past."

Everyone agreed. "Do you want me to walk you home?" Angie asked.

"No, stay here. You look exhausted," Jenna told her twin. "I won't be long. I think Libby and I will take a quick nap before dinner."

Ellie accompanied Jenna and her niece to the porch. "Text me when you get inside." She watched as they walked down the street until they were out of sight. The young woman checked the door locks when she went back into the house, even though she knew they were already fastened and bolted.

"Are you two hungry?" she asked Courtney and Rufus. "I can make sandwiches or heat up the soup I made yesterday."

Courtney shook her head. "I don't have much of an appetite."

Rufus agreed. "Maybe just some tea and toast. Comfort food."

"You got it." Ellie busied herself preparing the snacks.

"Let's go over the facts one more time," Mr. Finch suggested. "I find that helps me think."

As they sat around the kitchen table, Angie said,

"I'll start from the beginning. When Jenna was walking to the bake shop with Libby, she saw a suspicious dark-colored car parked across the street from our house. When the driver noticed them, he raced off."

The others nodded.

"Then later in the day when Jenna was working in her studio, she saw the ghost of a young woman who warned that danger was coming for our family."

"It was the same ghost Libby saw today who said Rufus and I shouldn't get married," Courtney added softly, her voice breaking.

Rufus put an arm around her shoulders. "But we are getting married, and nothing is going to stop us."

Angie gave them an encouraging smile and continued. "The other strange happening was the note and bracelet that Courtney received from the secret admirer."

"Whoever left that might be the person who was parked outside the house. It seems likely the admirer, ghost, and murder in Silver Cove are all connected," Ellie commented as she placed mugs of tea and plates with toast, butter, and jam on the table.

"Wait a second," Jenna said, "is the ghost we saw the spirit of the young woman killed in Silver Cove?"

Angie's eyes widened. "That's a very good question."

"I agree," said Mr. Finch. "We now have to ask what action does this individual intend to take next?"

No one had an answer. The old grandfather clock ticking in the hall seemed abnormally loud in the silence.

Finally, Rufus spoke up. "Well, he clearly wants to frighten Courtney and me, but we won't let him win. I say we carry on as planned with extra safety measures." He gave Courtney a reassuring smile.

Angie admired Rufus' resolve. Turning to Courtney she asked gently, "The wedding is only three weeks away. Are you sure you want to go through with it right now, with everything that's happening?"

Courtney lifted her chin. "Now more than ever. I won't let this creep ruin one of the happiest times of our lives." She clutched Rufus' hand tightly.

"Here, here," Mr. Finch said approvingly.

After Ellie and Angie prepared taco casserole for dinner, they spent the next two hours going over security strategies until Jenna returned with Libby. Gigi and her cousin took toys and played in the kitchen by the big windows, and having the joyful children close by lifted everyone's spirits.

Watching the little girls play with their barnyard animals, Angie was filled with love for her family. No matter what lay ahead, she was determined to protect the ones she cared about.

5

The next morning, Angie, Courtney, Rufus, and Mr. Finch drove the short distance to Silver Cove to meet Chief Martin at the crime scene. As they pulled up to the charming bungalow surrounded by tall trees, Angie gave Courtney a supportive smile. She knew this would be very hard for her sister.

Chief Martin greeted them solemnly at the front walk. "Thank you all for coming. I know it's never easy."

He led them past flower and vegetable gardens into the cozy house and then, to the living room where blood stained the area rug in several places. The chief explained that the victim was twenty-eight-year-old Barri Lewiston. She owned and ran a fabric and yarn store in the center of Silver Cove, where she also taught sewing and knitting classes. She was to marry her high school sweetheart Trevor Ralston, an accountant, the next day.

"There was no sign of forced entry," Chief Martin went on. "The coroner placed time of death between approximately 10 and 11 pm." His voice caught slightly on the last words.

Angie looked around the living room painted in warm earth tones and decorated with handmade quilts. She could envision Barri happily making plans for her wedding, blissfully unaware of the evil lurking outside. The image made bile rise in her throat.

Chief Martin told them Barri's parents, brother, and sister also live in Silver Cove and the family claimed the young woman had no enemies. "Why don't you walk around in here and have a look? I won't say any more so as not to influence you. Here are some surgical gloves to wear. If you pick up anything, put it back where you found it." He gave them plenty of time to walk through the house to see if they could sense any psychic impressions.

As the others wandered into the kitchen and down the hall to the bedrooms, Angie noticed Mr. Finch lingering in the living room.

His attention was focused on an overturned water glass on the floor near the hearth. Stepping closer, he reached a hand toward it hesitantly. Angie recognized the familiar faraway look in his eyes as he connected with the energy attached to the object.

After a long moment, he blinked slowly and turned to Angie. "I saw a glimpse of Barri's last moments. She was staring toward the kitchen, her eyes were wide with terror. The killer came in through the back of the house while she was in here. The door must have been unlocked." His voice was heavy with sadness.

When Angie placed a gentle hand on his shoulder, an odd energy swirled around her, but she couldn't sort out what it meant. Before she could say anything, Courtney and Rufus returned from exploring the bedrooms. Courtney's face was pale, and her eyes were red-rimmed.

"I keep seeing flickers of a dark, angry spirit," she said, her voice trembling slightly, "but the image is cloudy. I think my own anxiety is getting in the way and blocking my ability to sense anything."

Rufus wrapped an arm around her shoulders. "I picked up on intense fear and sensed Barri fighting back with all her strength." His jaw was taut with emotion.

Angie's heart ached for the young woman who'd had everything ahead of her. "It's so wrong that she lost her life just as it was starting," she said bitterly.

A tear rolled down Courtney's cheek. "She had family, friends, her own business. She was going to marry her high school sweetheart. The future was bright ... and then it was all ripped away." She turned tortured eyes on Angie. "I hope that isn't my fate, too."

Pulling Courtney into a fierce hug, Rufus said vehemently, "It won't be, I swear to you." Over her shoulder, the young man exchanged a grim look with Angie.

Angie told her sister, "You're going to be all right. Remember several Christmases ago when I was in danger and we didn't know where it might come from? We made it through that because we pulled together and all of you protected me. That's exactly what we're going to do this time."

Chief Martin surveyed the family with compassion. "I know this is difficult. You've all helped validate some of our theories about what happened that night. Barri did seem to be taken by surprise while in here hand sewing a quilt."

Angie looked down at the half-finished quilt

rumpled on the floor. She wanted to pick it up and have Ellie finish it for the young woman, but she knew they couldn't remove evidence.

Mr. Finch cleared his throat gruffly. "Sensing what went on in this place, I fear the person who did this is obsessed. We must be ready."

The others nodded, the weight of his words settling heavily over them. After a few more moments walking around the rooms again, they got ready to leave.

Courtney lingered in the doorway of the living room. "I wish we could have done something to help her," she whispered.

Rufus took her hand. "We'll make sure nothing bad happens to anyone else. That's the best way to honor her."

Courtney managed a small smile at him and nodded.

Angie knew scenes from the cozy home turned nightmare would stay seared in all their minds.

The group was subdued on the solemn ride back to Sweet Cove, each one lost in thought. Angie stared out the window as familiar shops and houses passed by. She realized suddenly how fragile things could be. *We all hang by a thread,* she thought.

When they arrived back at the Victorian, the rest of the family was waiting anxiously for news. As Courtney went inside supported by Rufus, Angie paused to look up at the graceful old house. It had weathered over a century of storms and still stood strong. She said a silent prayer their family would prove just as strong no matter what trouble lay ahead.

Inside, everyone gathered in the kitchen around the large farmhouse table to discuss what they had learned. Mr. Finch recounted his vision of Barri's final terrified moments.

"I felt something similar," Courtney said in a near whisper, "but I felt blocked by my anxiety."

As a heavy silence descended, Angie reached for her sister's hand, hating the cloud of dread hanging over the family at a time when things should be light and happy as they prepared for the upcoming wedding.

Finally, Ellie spoke up, her eyes troubled but resolute. "We don't know for certain the person who left the envelope for Courtney is behind this terrible crime in Silver Cove, but we probably have to assume it's the same person. Barri received notes of admiration and small gifts. It's the same thing that's being done to Courtney."

"There are similarities between Courtney and Barri," Josh pointed out. "They're close in age, they both own their own shops, and they have upcoming weddings."

"Could there be something specific that links Courtney and Barri?" Tom wondered aloud.

Jack asked Courtney, "You didn't know each other?"

The young woman shook her head.

"Maybe there's someone you both know or an activity you both did that might link you somehow to the killer," Jenna suggested.

"I'll start looking into that tomorrow," Angie promised.

"Okay, these are great ideas," Ellie said, "so let's put our heads together and make some more plans."

Her firm words shook Angie from her spiral of bleak thoughts. Ellie was right - they had to take action. They needed a plan. She met Mr. Finch's steady gaze.

"You're absolutely right, Ellie," Angie said. "We've overcome danger before and we'll do it again. We can't live under a shadow."

Mr. Finch gave a satisfied nod. "United, this family is unbreakable."

"But how do we fight someone we can't even

see?" Rufus said in frustration, raking a hand through his hair.

"We start by taking precautions to protect ourselves and each other, as the chief advised," Mr. Finch replied. "And we search for any small clue that could lead to finding the killer."

Angie considered this. "You're right. We start with practical measures - extra security and not traveling alone. And in the meantime, we could research to see if there have been any similar crimes, we can look for patterns, and we can dig for any possible clues or connections."

The faint spark of purpose began burning away at their feelings of helplessness. Angie continued, "We all have some different contacts who may have resources to help with finding clues. Jack and Rufus, you probably hear things through your legal circles. Tom has contacts in construction and renovation, and Josh has staff and visitors at the resort who might have seen or heard something about the murder in Silver Cove."

Her brothers-in-law looked thoughtful.

Jack said, "I'll discreetly ask around and see if this case rings any bells. There could be clues if we dig."

Tom nodded. "I'll do the same."

"I will as well," Josh told them.

Angie felt the momentum building as they came up with plans to arm themselves with knowledge. For the first time since the visit to Barri's house, she felt a sliver of hope.

Turning to Courtney and Rufus, she asked, "How are you two holding up through all this?" She knew having a ghost say they shouldn't be together had been chilling.

Courtney attempted a shaky smile. "We're hanging in there. I've been trying not to imagine that poor girl's face every time I close my eyes."

Rufus kept an arm snugly around her.

"Why don't you two go relax for a bit? We'll keep planning down here," Ellie suggested kindly.

As the couple moved off arm in arm, Angie called after them, "Everything will be okay. We're going to get to the bottom of this."

She prayed her words didn't ring false. Watching Courtney lean her head wearily on Rufus' shoulder as they headed for the staircase, Angie was reminded how love could be a source of strength, but also vulnerability.

Turning back to the others, she asked, "What else can we do to prepare and protect ourselves?"

They talked late into the night, plotting everything from home alarm systems to emergency contacts. Candles burned low as they worked together to strengthen their walls against threats.

When Angie and Josh finally crawled under the covers, they held hands until sleep pulled them under and away from their troubles ... for a few hours at least.

6

The next evening after dinner, Angie and Courtney sequestered themselves in the cozy study on the first floor of the Victorian house. They settled onto chairs, hoping to uncover any possible connection between Courtney and the murdered woman, Barri.

Angie powered up her laptop on the antique farmhouse desk, while Courtney grabbed a notebook and pen from the side table. The desk lamp cast a circle of warm light, illuminating the room lined with bookshelves full of novels, historic texts, and framed family photos.

"Let's start by making a list of similarities between you and Barri," Angie suggested. "That might reveal a common link or clue about why he fixated on you both."

Courtney tapped her pen on the notebook. "Well, we're around the same age – we're both in our late twenties. And we both own small shops in our towns."

"Good," said Angie, typing brief notes on the computer. "You both were engaged and had weddings planned this fall. You and Barri have blue eyes and different shades of blonde hair. You're similar in build and height, too."

Courtney nodded. "Oh, and we'd both been living here on the North Shore for several years after moving from the Boston area in our early twenties."

"Exactly, that's an important connection," Angie confirmed. She clicked open various social media sites to dig deeper into the dead woman's background.

Over the next hour, the two sisters carefully went through and compared their early lives and education. They discovered both had grown up in Boston but in different neighborhoods of the city. As children, they attended different elementary and high schools. Their friend groups and interests didn't seem to overlap much.

Angie sat back with a frustrated sigh. "On paper, your lives don't seem to intersect at all until moving to this area."

Courtney shook her head, setting down her notebook. "I know. I can't find any obvious thread tying us together before the stalking started." They were both silent for a few moments until Angie voiced the question that had been nagging at her.

"So, how on earth did this monster select his targets? His focus on you and Barri can't be purely random."

Courtney bit her lip, looking uneasy. "I guess it's possible he just noticed us around town if he lived nearby or something, but still, what made him fixate on us specifically?"

A thought crossed Angie's mind. "Do you think he could have been a customer at both of your shops? Maybe he visited the candy store or your art gallery and her fabric shop, and was attracted to both of you."

Courtney's blue eyes widened. "It does seem possible if he was a patron of both our businesses. He could have fixated on us that way over time. We probably talked to him, made friendly chit-chat with him."

Angie nodded slowly. "We'll need to dig more into that angle. We could try to spot anyone who might have visited both shops by reviewing security footage and sales records."

Courtney groaned, dropping her head into her hands. "That could take forever going through the endless hours of recordings. It would take an eternity to compare hours and hours of videos."

Angie nodded. "I know. I don't think it's humanly possible."

Straightening up, Courtney took a deep breath and met Angie's gaze. "Let's keep digging and trying to retrace both my and Barri's steps over the last year or so. Maybe we can narrow down possibilities for how he connected us."

Reenergized by their new direction, the sisters poured over archived shop sales records and social media posts late into the night, searching for any patrons, events, or activities that might have overlapped. But after hours of work yielded few promising leads, frustration and weariness grew.

Well past midnight, Angie finally closed her laptop with a tired sigh.

"There must be some intersection we're just not seeing," Angie said, rubbing her gritty eyes. "Somehow everything made twisted sense to him."

Courtney just shook her head despondently. She drew her knees up, staring into the darkened room as if it held unseen threats.

Angie moved to sit beside her sister on the

leather couch, wrapping an arm around her. "Hey, we're going to figure this out, I promise. We can't give up."

Courtney nodded, attempting a tremulous smile. "I know. I just wish we could uncover how he connected me to Barri. It all seems so random."

"We'll figure out his reasoning, however warped it might be," Angie assured her. Exhaustion was blurring their thought processes so the sisters decided to get some rest and approach the mystery again the next day with fresh eyes.

When Angie climbed into bed later, images from the long day swirled in her mind - photos of the vibrant young women building their lives, now clouded by sinister shadows. Maybe his choice of victims was as simple as the killer going into their shops and becoming mesmerized by the two young women. Was it possible the envelope for Courtney could be from someone other than the killer? Possible, but unlikely, Angie decided.

As she listened to Josh's gentle breathing beside her, she stared into the darkness of her room and thought about how the killer staked out his targets. She prayed they could stop him before he struck again.

Later that afternoon, Angie and Courtney drove to the Silver Cove neighborhood where Barri's fiancé Trevor lived. His large colonial house was set on a beautifully landscaped lot in an upscale part of town.

"Wow, pretty swanky digs for a guy in his twenties," Courtney commented as they walked up the brick path. "How can an accountant afford a place like this?"

"I think Chief Martin said Trevor owns his own firm," Angie replied. "I suppose he might have inherited the business. He must have a knack for maintaining and growing the accounting firm. Either way, he seems to be doing well for himself."

They rang the bell and a moment later Trevor opened the heavy wooden door. Angie was struck by how handsome he was with his athletic build, thick brown hair, and soft dark eyes. His appearance was marred by the raw grief that clung to him. Dark circles shadowed his eyes and his eyelids were rimmed red. He wore jeans and a rumpled sweater. He looked completely exhausted.

After quick introductions and offers of condolence for the loss of his fiancée, Trevor showed them to a richly appointed study. He gestured for them to take a seat on the leather sofa near the unlit fireplace.

"Chief Martin often asks us to follow up after his initial interview, in case someone has recalled something or might be able to provide more details that could help the investigation," Angie explained gently.

Trevor nodded, attempting to compose himself. "Anything you think could help catch who did this, I'll try my best to provide." His voice wavered with emotion.

Angie and Courtney exchanged a glance. They knew this process must be agonizing for him, yet Trevor seemed determined to stay composed and answer their questions thoroughly.

"You and Barri met in high school, correct?" Courtney began. "How did you first cross paths?"

The corner of Trevor's mouth lifted faintly at the memory. "We had a few classes together sophomore year. I saw her around but was too shy to talk to her at first. Then we finally connected over a group project in history class."

His smile faded and his eyes became distant. "We started dating shortly after that and have been together ever since."

Angie hesitated before asking the next question, though she knew it was necessary. "Did Barri have any known enemies or people who bore grudges against her?"

Trevor immediately shook his head. "Everyone loved Barri. She was the sweetest, kindest soul. She always got along with everyone." His voice cracked and he looked down, struggling to maintain composure.

After giving him a moment, Angie continued gently, "Wedding planning can sometimes be stressful. You two were handling everything smoothly? Any issues?"

Trevor swallowed hard. "Things were perfect between us. We rarely argued about anything. Planning our wedding day wasn't stressful at all." Trevor looked stricken and had to hold back his tears. The depth of his pain was almost palpable as he stared at his hands.

The sisters remained quiet until Trevor lifted his head. Angie offered him a box of tissues from the side table. He took a few, wiping his eyes roughly.

"I'm so sorry to have to ask these questions," Angie said softly.

"It's all right." Trevor took a steadying breath. "Anything that could help. Please, ask me anything."

Courtney gave him an encouraging nod. They continued probing gently about Trevor's impressions of Barri's relationships with family and friends, making sure to allow pauses when the strain overwhelmed him.

Trevor shared that Barri got along well with her parents, brother, and sister, though her sister Arlene could be controlling at times. Her brother liked to do his own thing and they weren't that close, but they got along fine.

"Did Barri have close friends?" Angie asked.

"Her closest friends were Lisa Monty and Jen Bates. They're both devastated by the loss."

"Did Barri have any issues with the women recently?"

"No issues at all. They got along well."

Courtney tried to lighten the mood a bit. "What were some of Barri's hobbies?

Trevor almost smiled. "She liked to run, play tennis, and hike in the state park. She liked to be active. She made quilts and enjoyed knitting. Have you seen some of her work? She was really an artist."

"We did see some of her quilts online. Was she happy running her own store?"

"It was a ton of work, but Barri always wanted

her own business. She was pleased with how well the shop was doing."

"Did she mention anyone strange interacting with her at the shop? Or anywhere else? Maybe someone who was too fixated on her?"

Trevor shook his head. "She never mentioned anything like that. I don't know who or why someone could have done this to her."

Nearly an hour passed before Angie and Courtney felt they had exhausted the questioning. As they prepared to leave, Angie touched the man's arm. "We can't thank you enough, and we're deeply sorry for your loss."

"Thank you." Trevor covered her hand with his own. "I pray you can help the police protect other women from the person who did this."

Outside, the sisters walked down the path to the car in thoughtful silence. The sun was dipping below the trees, casting the lovely neighborhood into shadow. Angie suppressed a shiver.

As they reached the car, Courtney turned to Angie. "That poor man. I hope reliving everything was worth it."

Climbing inside, Angie said grimly, "I know, but it had to be done. We're putting together the puzzle one piece at a time. What did you sense from him?"

"I thought he was telling the truth, but I do think he was glossing over parts of the relationship." Courtney shrugged. "Everyone gets annoyed with their partner sometimes. No one gets along perfectly all the time. Maybe he was trying to put their relationship into the best light possible. He might not have wanted to say anything negative."

"I agree with you." Angie looked back at the house. "If he had anything to do with Barri's death, he sure hid it well. Some people are good actors. I'm inclined to believe his grief, but I'm not yet ready to cross him off the suspect list."

As Angie pulled carefully onto the road that led back to Sweet Cove, the slanting sun momentarily blinded her. She braked hard, squinting into the glare. Were they moving toward light or fumbling into darkness? Shaking her head to clear it, Angie focused on the road ahead. The first step was making it home.

7

It was a sunny morning as Angie bustled about the Sweet Dreams Bake Shop wiping down tables, when she heard the door open and looked up with a smile to see her friend Francine breeze in, her emerald green eyes sparkling.

"There's my favorite baker," Francine called out. She and Angie exchanged a quick hug near the bakery counter. Angie admired the woman's stylish shoulder-length blonde hair and colorful sweater.

Francine was a stained glass artist and had a thriving business with a shop in Sweet Cove, a studio in Silver Cove, and an internet site to accept custom orders. The middle-aged woman was slim and trim and exuded a warm, positive energy.

Angie poured two cups of coffee, and they settled at a small bistro table near the big front window.

"How's your morning been so far?" Angie asked.

"Productive," Francine replied after sipping her coffee. "I finished a custom window piece for a client in Marblehead. How about you?"

"Steady as always." Angie glanced around her cozy domain, the smell of baked goods and the sound of chatting patrons filling the air.

Francine had lived in Silver Cove for years so Angie asked if she knew Barri Lewiston and Trevor Ralston.

Her friend gave her a sad look. "I did know Barri, not well, but I'd see her around at town events and meetings. She was a sweetheart. Her parents live a couple of streets over from me. I was devastated to hear what happened to her. I still can't believe it. The whole thing is so heartbreaking. She was to be married the next day. I guess you're working to help Chief Martin?"

Angie nodded grimly. Most locals knew she and her sisters occasionally consulted with the police on puzzling cases. "Do you know anything about Barri's family? Are you friendly with her parents?"

"They all must be devastated." Francine slowly shook her head. "I'm friendly with the parents, but not friends." She lowered her voice. "They're slightly unconventional."

"How so?"

"They're sort of like hippies from the sixties. They're harmless, but they often have a lot of people at the house, they play loud music, and they take drugs. They invited me to take part once, but that's not really my thing. They do seem very friendly and pleasant. They're interesting people. They have huge gardens behind the house."

"What do they do for a living?" Angie asked.

"I'm not sure. I know they dabble in art and music, but they don't have regular jobs. Maybe they have investments and savings, or maybe they received an inheritance. I don't know where their money comes from, but they seem well-off."

"What about the fiancé, Trevor Ralston?" Angie asked her friend. "Do you know much about him?"

Francine's face clouded and she took a moment to decide how to respond.

Angie's interest was piqued by her hesitation. "Please, if you have any impressions or insights, it could really help. We're trying to piece together what happened."

Francine took a few moments before replying. "Okay, but this stays between us. Well, go ahead and share what I tell you with Chief Martin if anything I say can be helpful in some way. I know Trevor's mother and I've heard from her that he has issues. He spends far beyond his means to sustain a lavish lifestyle. She worried he'd drag Barri into financial trouble."

Francine took a sip of her coffee. "Honestly, I never cared for Trevor. The young man loves glamour. He wants to be seen as successful, and wants all the material things to show he has money." She sighed softly. "He spends way beyond his limit. His mother told me he is in deep debt. She's been worried about him and his spending. He has a big house, an expensive car, and all the best things, from clothes to gadgets to furnishings for the house, but absolutely no savings."

"I wonder if Barri knew Trevor was spending beyond what he takes in," Angie said.

"Trevor's mother told me there was tension between him and Barri for the past six months, and it seemed to be escalating the closer they got to the wedding date. His mom liked Barri very much and was afraid she might decide not to marry Trevor."

"Really?" Angie was surprised. "Trevor painted a very rosy picture of his relationship with Barri. He didn't hint at any tension."

"Well, that's Trevor. He needs the world to see him as the best, the wealthiest, the luckiest in love." Francine shrugged. "I don't think he realized what a gem Barri was until she died and he understood what he'd lost."

Angie's mind raced, processing this new information. She recalled Courtney mentioning Trevor seemed to live quite extravagantly for an accountant.

"You wouldn't happen to know if Barri ever considered calling off the wedding?" Angie asked carefully.

"No idea." Francine lifted one shoulder. "Trevor's mother did hint that Barri might be having doubts. Like I said, it's all just conjecture, but I had a sense their relationship might have been strained, despite the happy face Trevor puts on."

Angie nodded slowly. "I really appreciate you letting me know all of this." She looked straight at Francine. "Did you know Barri had a stalker?"

Francine's eyes went wide. "A stalker?" She stared at her friend. "What on earth?"

Angie explained how Barri had received notes and small gifts from a secret admirer. "The police think the admirer might have been the killer."

"How awful." Francine's hand went to her throat.

"What a nightmare. Do the police have any suspects?"

"I don't think so. It's still early," Angie went on, "but now Courtney has a secret admirer who left her a note and a handmade bracelet."

Francine's jaw dropped. "Oh, no," she whispered. "Is it the same person?"

"We don't know, but the police are treating it like it is ... just to be cautious." Angie shook her head. "Courtney doesn't know it yet, but Josh is interviewing security personnel. We're thinking of hiring one person to guard her during the day, and one for the evening duty. Josh would like to hire four people to switch up their schedules so they can have off days."

"That's a huge expense."

Angie nodded. "Josh and I will do anything to keep Courtney safe. It's temporary. Once the killer is in custody, she won't need protection anymore."

"Will Courtney go along with it?" Francine knew the young woman was fiercely independent.

"It will take some convincing, I'm sure." Angie sighed.

After discussing the case for a few more minutes, their conversation turned to Francine's latest glasswork projects and Courtney and Rufus' upcoming wedding.

The bakery's door opened and several customers entered. The two friends exchanged a smile as Angie stood to return to work.

"Thanks for stopping in and for the helpful chat," Angie said warmly.

After Francine departed, Angie found herself preoccupied as she waited on patrons and restocked displays. If Trevor had been leaning on Barri financially, it might explain why he portrayed their relationship as idyllic during the interview. He may have even come to resent Barri's stability.

Angie's instincts told her this avenue needed further exploration. She would tell Chief Martin what she learned as soon as she closed up shop for the day.

Later that evening, Ellie and Angie joined Jenna in the jewelry studio at the back of the Victorian to help with packaging online orders. As they carefully wrapped necklaces, earrings, and bracelets for shipping, the conversation turned to Courtney's troubling situation.

"I just can't understand why a ghost would warn that Courtney and Rufus shouldn't be together," Ellie remarked as she nestled a pair of copper earrings into a velvet jewelry box.

Jenna finished tying a satin bow around another gift box before responding. "I know. It doesn't make any sense. Those two are perfect for each other."

Angie placed an order into a shipping envelope, a slight furrow in her brow. "There's a reason the spirit gave that ominous message, but what could it be?"

Ellie asked, "Is Courtney in danger because of someone she knows or met in the candy shop or the art gallery? How can we protect her?"

"Is Rufus in danger as well?" Jenna questioned. "The ghost didn't seem to have the energy to stay visible to me for long. Maybe the message was cut off because the ghost couldn't stay long enough to finish the communication."

"I wish we had more information." Angie shook her head as she reached for another gift box.

The sisters were silent for a few moments; the only sound was of the crinkling of tissue paper and scissors snipping ribbons. Finally, Jenna looked up.

"Maybe we should try contacting the ghost again,

see if we can get more details. Maybe if I reach out, she'll return."

Ellie appeared doubtful. "Do you really think the spirit would come forth and communicate with you?"

"It's worth a try," Jenna said. "I'd like to at least attempt making contact."

Angie considered the idea while absently twisting the wedding ring on her finger. "I agree it couldn't hurt. Should we leave you alone to try to summon her?"

"No, stay with me. I think it would work better with all our energy working together." Jenna's expression brightened. "Let's do it right now. We can clear some space in the center of the room and I'll light some candles to set the mood."

Soon the three sisters were seated in a small circle on the hardwood floor, surrounded by flickering candles. With hands linked, they centered their minds and slowed their breathing. Jenna softly asked the spirit to come forth.

After several long, silent moments, she called out gently, "We seek your wisdom and guidance about the danger you foretold. Please help us understand how to protect our sister."

The candles continued to dance, casting

wavering shadows over the women's faces as they waited, but no ghostly presence announced itself.

"Anything?" Ellie asked.

"Nothing." Jenna's voice was full of disappointment.

Finally, Angie gave a subtle shake of her head.

Jenna sighed but nodded in understanding. Dropping their linked hands, the sisters rose from the floor.

"Maybe it will work next time," Ellie offered as she began gathering the candles to put out the flames.

Jenna pulled her sweater around her. "I could sense a spiritual presence nearby, but it seemed reluctant to fully manifest."

"Do you think we need assistance to make contact?" Angie asked. "We could talk to Orla and get her input."

At nearly seventy years of age, Orla Abel was a friend and an intuitive medium the sisters occasionally consulted when they needed advice. They decided Jenna's ghostly vision could use the woman's expertise.

"Hopefully, Orla can shed some light on why the spirit is warning against Courtney's marriage," Ellie said.

Jenna nodded, looking relieved they had a plan. "I was hoping to handle this ourselves, but I think you're right, we need Orla's help."

As the trio finished packaging the orders and tidied up the studio, Angie felt heartened by the reminder they had allies they could call on. With Orla's guidance, maybe the ghost's message would finally make sense and they could think of ways to protect their youngest sister.

For Courtney's sake, Angie prayed they could persuade the reluctant spirit to come out from the shadows and communicate with them. Silently, she repeated Mr. Finch's words - forewarned was forearmed.

8

It was late afternoon when Courtney returned to the Victorian after a long day working at the candy shop. She was looking forward to unwinding with her sisters over a homemade meal, but as Courtney came up the front walk, she noticed a small wooden box sitting on the porch railing.

Her footsteps slowed in apprehension. It was a pretty box with a small envelope attached. Her name was written across it in the elaborate script she recognized all too well. Courtney's stomach dropped as her hands balled into fists. She didn't have to open it to know this was another gift from her mysterious admirer.

Snatching up the box with trembling hands, the young woman hurried inside, calling out for her sisters. She found Angie and Jenna chatting with Mr. Finch in the cozy kitchen. The comforting smells of dinner cooking did little to ease her rattled nerves.

"You need to see this right now," Courtney said, dropping the box onto the farmhouse table with a thud. "I just found it outside."

The others stared at the package warily as Courtney explained where she had discovered it. Dread crept down Angie's spine like icy fingers.

Not again.

Jenna reached for the envelope with Courtney's name penned on it, but stopped with her hand in the air. "We shouldn't touch it. The police might want to dust for fingerprints."

Using a pencil to slide the note from the envelope, Mr. Finch saw the same flowing script as the earlier note, and he read the words aloud:

"My dearest Courtney,

Another small token of my growing affection to show you how treasured you are."

As Mr. Finch continued reading the chilling message, Courtney visibly shuddered at the obsessive words and Angie felt her anger rising into her throat like bile. This was no harmless crush.

"This is really scaring me," Courtney said in a small voice, hugging herself tightly. "He knows where I live. It's like he's watching my every move, all the time."

Mr. Finch's face was grave, his eyes clouded with concern. "Clearly this individual feels emboldened if he left this on our porch in broad daylight. Such a brazen escalation means we must be extremely cautious."

"Should we open the box?" Jenna asked uncertainly.

Courtney immediately shook her head. "I don't even want to look at it. Just throw the whole thing in the trash," she pleaded.

"But," Angie said, "we need to examine it first. There could be trace evidence that could help identify him."

Donning cleaning gloves from under the sink, Angie carefully lifted the ornate hinged lid. Inside lay an antique gold locket on a delicate chain. It looked to be quite old and valuable. She suspected it was stolen. Looking at it, her anger reignited, pulsing hotly through her veins.

"Jenna, will you please call Chief Martin?" she requested. "See if they can send someone over to pick this up to dust for prints and analyze for clues."

As Jenna stepped to the side to call the station,

Angie turned to her distressed sister. She hated feeling so powerless to help Courtney.

"Josh wants to hire private bodyguards to keep an eye on things. There would be someone with you 24-7. Would you be okay with that?" she asked. "Just until this psycho is caught."

Courtney's eyes filled with tears of frustration. "I just want my life back. I should be happy, enjoying my engagement, getting ready for my wedding, not living in fear." She swiped at the tears angrily. "Instead, I'm constantly looking over my shoulder and jumping at every sound. I really don't want security people around me. It would be a constant reminder that I'm in danger. I'm never alone; I'm here with the family, I'm with Rufus, and there are plenty of people around when I'm at work. I appreciate the kind offer, but I'm not ready to do that just yet."

Angie wrapped her sister in a fierce, protective hug. "This isn't how it's going to be forever. The police will catch him." She hoped the determination in her voice masked her own simmering fear.

Over Courtney's shoulder, she exchanged a grim, worried look with Mr. Finch. This admirer appeared fully obsessed, circling ever closer to his prey. They needed to halt his twisted attention before it was too late.

Just then, Ellie walked in the back door carrying a couple of market bags. Her cheery expression faded immediately when she saw Courtney's distress and the disturbing gift box on the table.

"What's happened?" she asked, hurrying over with concern etched on her face.

Once they'd updated her on the latest threat, Ellie's eyes flashed with anger and her jaw clenched. "This has to end," she declared. "We know this monster killed that poor girl in Silver Cove. He isn't going to harm anyone in our family."

Mr. Finch held up a hand cautiously. "You're quite right, my dear. We must remain clear-headed to face this problem. Why don't we ask our neighbors if they have door cameras? Perhaps this person will show up on security video as he places the note and box on our porch."

Ellie said, "We should have a door cam installed at the front and back of the house."

"And on the candy shop and the art gallery," Courtney added. "The more cameras, the better."

Angie nodded, keeping a steadying arm around Courtney. She wished desperately that she could shield her sister from this nightmare, but the harsh truth was that until the stalker was stopped for good, none of them were truly safe.

As Jenna turned to the family members to say the police were sending a car right over, Angie caught a glimpse of Euclid and Circe, observing silently from the hallway. Their wise, watchful eyes seemed to track every movement. Angie knew they were listening to every word.

Staring down at the wooden box on the table, Angie hoped the police would find a clue that would finally expose the admirer's identity. Then they could turn the tables on the monster and put him away for good. She longed for the day when her sister could recover her sense of safety and joy.

Courtney took a deep breath and turned to Angie. "Remember when Jenna saw that vision of you several years ago at Christmastime?"

Jenna flinched at the memory.

"I remember." Angie smiled. "It's not a good memory, except for one thing."

"Jenna saw a little girl in her vision," Courtney said with a smile. "And that little girl was Gigi. Jenna saw your daughter before you were even pregnant."

"But before that, Jenna saw me in a coffin," Angie said.

Jenna shook her head. "It was awful. I was so afraid you were going to die."

"How did you get through that, Angie?" Courtney asked her oldest sister. "How did you not go crazy with fear that you were going to be killed?"

Angie blinked as she thought back to that Christmas. "I was deathly afraid, but I decided my fear wasn't going to run my life. I was going to do everything possible to live. I wanted to see my daughter one day." She glanced around at the people in the room. "I had all of you with me, and together, that kept me alive."

Courtney smiled. "Then that's what I'm going to do. I'm going to fight like heck, and when I can't fight anymore, then all of you will pick me up and fight like heck for me."

9

The next day, the sisters gathered with Mr. Finch and Orla Abel in the cozy family room of the Victorian home to discuss how best to combat the ominous threats facing them. A fire crackled soothingly in the hearth as the group settled into the overstuffed armchairs and sofas, mugs of tea and a plate of Angie's freshly baked mini cupcakes on the coffee table before them.

Orla carefully surveyed each young woman's face. In her early seventies, the intuitive psychic possessed a vigorous energy and a sharp mind.

"Now then," Orla began, "tell me everything that's occurred so I'm up to speed."

Over the next half hour, the sisters took turns filling in Orla on the disturbing chain of events - the murder in Silver Cove, Jenna's and Libby's visions of the ghostly warning, and the secret admirer's escalating gifts and notes to Courtney.

Orla listened intently, absently stroking Euclid and Circe, who had curled up next to her. When the recap was finished, the woman let out a heavy sigh and shook her head.

"You all seem to attract trouble like honey attracts bears," she remarked wryly. "But we'll figure a way out of this mess, never you fear."

Courtney managed a little smile, comforted by Orla's confidence.

"Have you made any headway contacting the spirit again?" Orla asked Jenna. "We need to understand why she's cautioning against Courtney and Rufus being together."

Jenna's face fell and she shook her head regretfully. "I haven't picked up anything further from her since that first brief appearance, but I think the ghost is Barri, the murdered young woman from Silver Cove."

"Hmm, you're probably right." Orla took a sip of tea. "She may have come to warn Courtney because she was a victim of the same stalker."

Turning to Angie, Orla asked, "What about you,

dear? Have you been able to pick up any psychic impressions related to all this?"

Angie looked thoughtful. "I've had a few intuitive nudges now and then, but no definite visions or insights."

Orla set down her teacup. "Okay. I'd like both you and Jenna to start working closely with Mr. Finch again." She turned to the older man. "Victor, have you been painting or sketching recently?"

Mr. Finch nodded. "I've been sketching in my notebook, working on some ideas for a series of watercolors."

"Good. Jenna and Angie should sit with you each day to look through your sketches. Some insights or visions may come to them. We must uncover whatever information the spiritual realms can provide."

Jenna still appeared hesitant, so Orla continued gently, "I know it's frightening, but practice and training will help you learn to interpret the signs correctly. You don't want to close yourself off to the spirit world."

Mr. Finch gave Jenna an encouraging smile. "Whenever you're ready, we can start slow. We can go over just a few sketches at a time. I have the utmost faith in you."

Bolstered by their reassurances, Jenna managed

a small, brave nod. "You're right - we need any advantage we can get. I'll try."

"Excellent." Orla briskly brushed a few cat hairs from her skirt and picked up her tea once more. "Now then, a protection circle would also be wise. Why don't we get together in a couple of days and we'll gather a few others to join us?"

Seeing Jenna's brow furrow, Orla held up a staying hand. "I know what you're thinking and before you ask, yes, I think young Libby should participate in a circle with the family for practice but she doesn't have to come when we gather together."

Jenna looked startled. "But she's not quite four years old. Isn't she too young for something so serious?"

Orla shook her head, looking thoughtful. "On the contrary, I think that remarkable little girl's gifts could be quite helpful. The paranormal is natural for her ... it's part of who she is, and this would nurture her talents."

Mr. Finch nodded slowly in agreement. "Orla makes an excellent point. Early training would be very beneficial for Miss Libby. She has wonderful gifts. We have to help her soar."

Jenna still seemed uncertain but finally nodded.

"Well, if you both feel it's all right, I can try explaining it to her."

"Wonderful. That's settled then." Orla finished her tea and carefully transferred a sleeping cat from her lap to the sofa as she stood.

"There are a couple more ideas I want to develop a bit further," she told the group. "I'll be in touch soon about the details."

After thanking Orla for her help and guidance, the sisters walked her out to the stone path that led from the back of the Victorian, through a grove of trees, and into the backyard of the house she shared with her husband Mel. The fresh air and moonlight lifted their spirits after the intense session.

As Orla walked away along the lighted path, Angie turned to Courtney and Jenna with an optimistic smile. "That went well. I think we have a solid plan taking shape."

Courtney took a deep breath and let it out slowly. "I hope you're right. My nerves are too rattled to gauge much at the moment." She attempted a smile.

Pulling her sister into a hug, Angie said firmly, "Try not to worry. Orla is the perfect advisor for this, and we have more allies than you realize. It's going to be okay."

But as Angie held her sister close, she couldn't

prevent a cold tendril of fear from creeping down her own spine. The stalker was terrifying.

Over the next two days, Jenna spent time gently preparing her daughter for the upcoming protection ritual. Though she kept the details minimal for Libby's young mind, Jenna was amazed at how easily the child grasped the basic concepts.

"We're going to help keep the bad shadows away," Libby summarized confidently after Jenna's careful explanation.

Jenna smiled and kissed her brow. "Exactly right, sweetheart." Her heart swelled with love and pride.

Meanwhile, Angie and Mr. Finch prepared the backyard for a practice session with just the family, hanging windchimes and crystals from tree branches and laying out candles around the stone firepit.

As dusk fell on the appointed evening, Tom, Jack, Rufus, and Josh met the women, Mr. Finch, Libby, and the cats in the garden and formed a loose circle.

Mr. Finch guided them to visualize a glowing perimeter of protective light surrounding the group. Then they joined hands, and he led them in chanting words of safety and security.

All the while, little Libby sat calmly in the grass

beside her mother with one cat on either side of her, with her eyes closed and lips moving silently along with the chant. Jenna was struck again by her daughter's natural attunement to the ritual.

As the rite drew to a close, a tangible sensation of comfort and security enveloped them. Their spirits felt bolstered and their nerves soothed. Mr. Finch gave Courtney a kind, approving smile across the dwindling flames.

Later that night as she tucked Libby into bed, Jenna leaned down and whispered, "You did a beautiful job tonight, sweetheart. I'm so proud of you."

Libby gave her mother a sleepy but confident smile. "The bad shadows won't get Auntie Courtney now, Mama. We have our magic light."

Jenna's heart swelled, knowing her daughter spoke the truth.

Unable to sleep, Angie slipped out of bed and padded quietly downstairs to the kitchen to make herself a cup of chamomile tea. The old house creaked and settled around her as she waited for the kettle to boil.

Soon after preparing her tea, Angie heard soft

footsteps and turned to see Courtney entering the kitchen in her pajamas.

"Couldn't sleep either?" Angie asked.

Courtney shook her head, mussing her already tousled hair. "My brain won't shut off tonight."

Angie patted the chair beside her. "I'll make you a nice cup of tea."

Soon the two sisters were seated at the table sipping tea and chatting softly. The familiar kitchen lit only by the moonlight streaming through the windows lent a dreamlike quality to their midnight chat.

After nearly a half hour passed, Angie noticed intermittent flashing lights outside the window over the back sink. She stiffened, the hairs on her arms standing on end. What was that?

Courtney followed her gaze, gasping when she saw the odd lights blinking again from the backyard. Fear jolted through them as they exchanged an anxious glance.

Moving to the window, Angie noticed two familiar forms emerge from the bushes - the cats! Relief flooded through her. If Euclid and Circe were at ease, then there was no danger to worry about.

Peering closer out the window, Angie could just make out Mr. Finch's figure standing near the pergola. Curiosity replaced her fear. "What are the cats and Mr. Finch doing out there at this hour?"

"Let's go see what's going on," Courtney suggested, already heading for the back door. Mystified, Angie followed close behind.

The security lights illuminated Mr. Finch in the center of the yard as the sisters approached. He appeared to be alone.

"Mr. Finch, what are you doing out here?" Angie called gently so as not to startle him.

The older gentleman turned to them looking a bit sheepish. "Oh, hello, Miss Angie, Miss Courtney. You caught me out on one of our ... training exercises."

"Training exercises?" Courtney repeated in confusion.

Before Mr. Finch could explain further, a sweat-drenched figure emerged from the trees – it was Rufus. The young man had a huge grin on his flushed face.

"Rufus!" Courtney exclaimed. "What on earth are you doing with Mr. Finch?"

Rufus chuckled, grabbing a towel the older man handed him to mop his brow. "I guess we've been found out."

Just then, Jack and Tom also appeared from the

bushes sporting dark clothing and flak jackets. In a moment, Ellie came out from the trees at the back of the property with her long blonde hair pulled back in a ponytail.

"Ellie's here, too?" Courtney turned her wide eyes on Mr. Finch. "Would someone please explain what's going on here?"

Mr. Finch stepped forward. "My apologies for the secrecy. We've been, shall we say, running some night maneuvers for Rufus and the others to hone their skills. We're running training experiences in different places at night. Everyone needs to be ready should the need arise. We asked Ellie to join us due to her telekinesis skills. She is able to send a weapon toward Rufus without him seeing her."

Comprehension dawned on the sisters. "Oh, combat training," said Angie.

Rufus wiped his face with the towel. "Mr. Finch is instructing me on defensive and offensive moves and behaviors. The other guys act like attackers I have to take out. Euclid and Circe try to sneak up on me. We work on different techniques to strengthen my fire power," Rufus elaborated.

Jack shrugged, looking full of energy. "It's been oddly fun taking part in these midnight exercises all over town. We've been on the beach, in the state forest, by the lake, and here in the yard. We try to do it every two or three nights."

Ellie came over and slipped her hand through her husband's arm. "It's great fun actually. I feel like a warrior."

"And Rufus is getting really good with his fire power," Tom remarked, clapping the younger man on the back.

Courtney hurried over to hug Rufus. "You've been doing all this extra training to keep me safe?" She blinked back tears, deeply moved.

"I'll do whatever it takes to protect you," Rufus vowed, rubbing her cheek. "Mr. Finch is an excellent instructor."

Mr. Finch inclined his head modestly at the praise. "We normally train from midnight to one. The darkness and element of surprise pushes everyone to stay sharp."

"Thank you so much," Courtney told them. "I love you all for doing this."

Angie shook her head in amazement. She never ceased to be touched by the lengths her family would go to help each other. "Where's Josh? Is he helping?"

"We take turns," Tom explained. "We switch off. It's Josh's night off."

Angie said, "Well, since we're up and awake, let's see how you practice."

The women watched the men, Ellie, and the cats run the next sequence, and they clapped and hooted when it was over.

"Why don't Courtney and I join in your last exercise tonight?" Angie proposed.

Mr. Finch looked delighted. "A wonderful idea. Let me explain the roles."

Soon the expanded group was in position around the yard. At Mr. Finch's signal, the mock attack sequence commenced. Though initially anxious, Angie found herself getting into the spirit of the drill, dramatically lobbing some "threats" at Rufus.

By the end, everyone was laughing and breathless. Rufus swept Courtney up in his arms, gazing at her with admiration. "You were incredible, love. And those flames were really shooting from my fingers tonight."

"No wonder I think you're so hot." Courtney smiled and kissed him. "I have my very own superhero."

As they all headed inside for a late-night snack, Angie's heart swelled with love for her family.

Protecting each other was the surest shield against the dangers they faced.

Later that night as she finally crawled back under the covers, Angie fell asleep with a soft smile, the image of Rufus whirling in the yard with his hands blazing flashing behind her eyelids.

10

It was early evening on a sunny Saturday when the Roseland sisters gathered in the backyard garden of the Victorian home to finalize the details of Courtney and Rufus' upcoming wedding ceremony. A sense of hope and happiness filled the air as they discussed the details.

"We should set up the chairs in rows facing the big oak tree," Ellie suggested, pointing across the lawn. "It will make such a beautiful backdrop."

The others agreed as they envisioned the tree's branches spreading above the couple while they exchanged vows.

"Ooh, we can decorate the aisle posts with roses and ribbons," Angie added eagerly.

As they talked over options, the women paced

around visualizing the layout. Courtney could see everything coming together.

"Rufus and I will stand under the oak arch to say our vows," she described. "His best men can stand to his right, and my three maids of honor will be to my left."

"Perfect," said Jenna. " Angie and Josh, me and Tom, then Ellie and Jack can walk down the aisle ahead of you and Mr. Finch."

They walked to the side of the yard and Angie pointed. "We can have the musicians sit here under the big beech tree."

Ellie told them, "If the weather isn't going to be great, I have a company ready to come the day before to put up white tents so everyone will be sheltered, but maybe we should have them set up no matter the forecast. It can be hot sitting out in the sun."

Angie added, "After the ceremony, formal pictures will be taken while the guests are shuffled by trolleys down to the yacht, where there will be drinks, hors d'oeuvres, and music waiting for them."

"I don't know how I'd pull this off without you three." Courtney beamed and linked arms with her sisters as excitement filled her heart. "This is really happening - I'm marrying the man I've always loved."

After a joyful group hug, Angie glanced at her watch. "We better get ready if we want to meet the guys on time."

They were heading into Coveside to meet Courtney's fiancé Rufus, along with Josh, Jack, Tom, Mr. Finch, and his girlfriend Betty for dinner on the yacht. Combined with wedding planning, it was shaping up to be an ideal day.

After quick showers and changing into casual sundresses, the four sisters piled into Ellie's SUV and headed down to Coveside toward the marina. Courtney gazed happily out the window as familiar storefronts slid by until the glittering expanse of Sweet Cove Harbor came into view.

Soon they had parked the car and were strolling down to the docks, weaving through the crowds. Courtney spotted the sleek white yacht, its polished wood and gleaming accents looking almost regal beside the other yachts and weathered fishing boats. She picked up her pace, grinning, when she noticed Rufus waving from the rear deck. His eyes had lit up at the sight of her.

Once up onto the boat, everyone exchanged hugs and settled into easy conversation as Rufus popped open a bottle of champagne. "To happy days ahead for all of us. And to Angie and Josh for providing the most beautiful wedding reception venue ever," he toasted, smiling lovingly at Courtney.

"Cheers to that," Jack chimed in as they clinked glasses. The bubbly liquid tasted especially good.

The Roseland women told the others about how the garden of the Victorian would be set up.

Angie said, "Once Courtney told us what she and Rufus wanted, we made a few suggestions and walked around the yard imagining how it all would look."

"It's going to be beautiful," Courtney said.

"We can't wait," Tom smiled. "I do love a wedding."

Sitting on a comfortable sofa watching the gathering, Euclid and Circe trilled in delight.

As the yacht motored out of the harbor, the group sat down to dinner and feasted on shrimp cocktails, clam chowder, crab cakes, and salad while chatting happily about the wedding plans.

Courtney sighed, thinking she couldn't be more thrilled to be surrounded by family, her true love, and the shimmering ocean. It seemed almost too wonderful to be real after the upset of the past week.

When the meal was over, the others listened to

music and enjoyed after-dinner drinks while Courtney, Rufus, Angie, and Josh sat together in the salon to discuss the final details and arrangements for the reception.

Angie had a notebook on the table in front of her. "So, after the ceremony, the guests will be shuttled down to the boat. There will be music, drinks, and appetizers for them to enjoy. When the rest of us arrive, we'll all be introduced as we come onto the yacht, and then we'll have cocktail hour. When we're called to dinner in the dining room, the band will play the song for your first dance. After the meal, Courtney will dance with Mr. Finch for the 'adopted-father-daughter dance,' and Rufus and his mother will dance together."

"Sounds good," the couple replied.

"Then everyone will be invited to the dance floor to join in," Angie explained. "Is that how you want it to go?"

"Everything sounds great." Courtney nodded.

Angie turned to the back of the notebook and described the dinner tables set-up and where the floral arrangements would be placed. They decided on a mix of musical styles for dancing under the stars on the yacht deck.

"We love it," Courtney told her sister.

"It's more than we could ever hope for." Rufus thanked Angie and Josh.

The couples rejoined their family and friends, and too soon, the captain was steering the vessel back toward the docks as the setting sun cast rippling gold trails across the water.

Hand in hand, Courtney and Rufus strolled to the bow of the ship and when their eyes met, she knew he was savoring the moment as much as she was.

"Just think, in a couple of short weeks we'll be starting our married life together," Rufus murmured, pulling her closer.

Courtney smiled up at him, her heart brimming with love and excitement for their future voyage. "I know. I can hardly believe the wedding day is almost here."

Her smile faltered a bit as a worrying thought intruded. "That's part of why I wanted to get away from the others, just the two of us, for a bit. There's been so much going on."

Rufus stared into Courtney's eyes. "What is it?"

Her eyes were downcast. "I just wonder some-times if we're doing the right thing going through with the wedding right now. With everything that's happening..." She trailed off miserably.

Tipping her chin up, Rufus smiled at her. "Courtney, look at me. Nothing could make me change my mind about marrying you. Stalkers and ghosts aren't going to scare me off."

Courtney gave a half-hearted laugh at his fervent tone. "I know. I just worry for your safety with this stalker stuff going on. And then there are the warnings about us not being together." She felt tears gathering.

"Hey, now, none of that." Rufus thumbed a stray tear from her cheek. "We can't let fear rule our lives. I knew when I met you that you were my one and only. I don't care what ghosts say about us, and I'm not going to cower in front of a stalker. I love you, Courtney, and I'll be by your side ... now and forever."

Courtney smiled up at him. "How did I ever find you?"

Rufus grinned. "Just lucky, I guess."

As the sun continued its descent toward the sea, Courtney and Rufus rejoined the family, and the group lingered over slices of pineapple upside-down cake and Angie's shortbread cookies, laughing about fond memories of childhood misadventures.

At last, the captain angled the vessel back into its berth and Courtney sighed, wishing she could hold onto the moment a little longer - the gentle rocking of the boat, the peals of laughter, Rufus' strong hand in hers.

After they'd disembarked and shared hugs on the dock, Mr. Finch and Betty, and Josh, Tom, Jack, Rufus, and the cats walked to the lot to get the cars. Courtney and her sisters put on light sweaters as they set off down the main street to look at the shops before heading back home.

Turning down one of the side streets with the ocean spread before them, Angie looped her arm through Courtney's. "I can't remember the last time I saw you looking so happy," she remarked.

Courtney smiled. "Everything just feels so right. The wedding planning, time with all of you, my amazing fiancé."

Up ahead, the lighthouse beam swept over the darkening water. As they walked, the four sisters fell into easy conversation about floral arrangements, music choices, and Ellie's finishing touches on the bridal dress.

Courtney thought back to the pleasant evening on the boat and how that graceful ship would carry her to the next leg of life's adventure. And she would embark on that trip with her anchor - the man who saw her heart and vowed to always guard it.

11

When Chief Martin asked if a couple of the Roselands could go talk with Barri's sister Arlene Lewiston, Courtney asked to bow out.

"I'm feeling good right now and I don't want to be pulled back into thinking about stalkers and killers, or how Barri died right before her wedding," Courtney said as she finished her breakfast before heading off to work at the art gallery.

Angie said, "I can go speak to Arlene, but I'd like someone to come with me."

"I'd like to go, but I have to work in the candy shop all day until nearly 8 pm," said Mr. Finch. "I believe Miss Jenna has meetings with retail shops in Salem and Newburyport today about her jewelry line."

Ellie was preparing a cart with breakfast items including French toast bake for the B & B guests. "I can go with you later this afternoon. I'd like to hear what Barri's sister has to say about the death."

When Angie closed the bake shop for the day, she and Ellie drove to Arlene Lewiston's house in Silver Cove. The pretty Cape-style house set back on a large piece of land near the state forest was surrounded by flower gardens.

"Look at the gardens." Ellie admired the beds of blooms winding past a white fence. "They're beautiful. I wonder if Arlene takes care of them herself."

Angie rang the front doorbell, and Barri's sister opened it a few minutes later.

"You must be the consultants Chief Martin sent." Arlene was of average height with a few extra pounds on her frame. Her hair was dark blonde and reached her collarbone. Her eyes looked at the two Roseland sisters with suspicion.

Angie and Ellie introduced themselves and offered condolences for the loss of Arlene's sister.

Despite Arlene appearing slightly uncooperative when they met at the front door, she welcomed them inside to a beautifully decorated home. They settled in the living room to talk.

"I can't believe Barri is gone," Arlene told them as she poured ice tea into three glasses.

Ellie asked, "How would you describe your relationship with your sister?"

"We got along fine. Sure, we had disagreements, but we always respected each other."

"What was Barri like?"

Arlene's eyes widened. "Barri was the favored one. Our parents would poo-poo that bit of information, but it's a fact. Everyone loved Barri. She was a ray of sunshine. She was kind, smart, creative, athletic. She had a good mind for business. Her shop did well; she had lots of return customers and followers on social media."

"What did she post on social media?" Angie asked.

"About her shop, what projects she was creating, short reels with helpful instructions for knitting or sewing projects."

Arlene took a long sip of iced tea before continuing. "Barri was also super sociable - always chatting with customers or joining some club or class. I think she knew most everyone in town."

"It sounds like she was very well-liked," Ellie said. "Do you know of anyone who would have wished her harm or held a grudge against her?"

Frowning, Arlene traced a fingertip around the condensation on her glass. "I honestly can't think of a soul who didn't like Barri. She just had this light about her, you know? She made people feel noticed and special."

Angie and Ellie exchanged a subtle glance. They needed to delve deeper beneath this saintly facade people used to describe Barri.

"Even the closest relationships can be complex," Angie noted gently. "Did you two ever experience any notable tensions or disagreements over the years?"

Arlene sighed, sinking back into the plush sofa cushions. "I mean, we had minor spats now and then when we were kids, like all siblings, but nothing serious as adults. I never wanted any harm to come to my sister, and I certainly didn't kill her." She shook her head, almost incredulous. "How could anyone intentionally hurt someone so vivacious and kind? She was the sweetest person."

"We understand this is very difficult to process," Ellie said in a soothing tone. "What about romantically? Did Barri have any jealous exes or signs of problems with her fiancé?"

At the mention of Trevor, Arlene's gaze sharpened and her mouth tightened. "Now that pompous, arrogant jerk is another story entirely. He was completely wrong for Barri in every way."

Angie leaned forward with interest, making eye contact with Ellie for a split second. This was the first crack in the pristine image Arlene had painted of her sister's life. "You seem to have a strong dislike for Trevor. Can you tell us more about that?"

Arlene flushed slightly, seeming to regret her candid words. "Just that they didn't suit one another at all, in my opinion. But Barri was convinced he was 'the one,' God knows why." She rolled her eyes in exasperation.

"Was there something specific about Trevor you found objectionable as a partner for your sister?" Ellie pressed gently.

Fiddling absently with a throw pillow, Arlene considered her response. "I know I shouldn't speak ill of my dead sister's fiancé, but Trevor is arrogant and entitled. He's always flashing his money around and treated Barri more like a trophy than a real partner. She deserved so much better."

This matched the gossip from Francine about Trevor's flamboyant show of wealth and precarious finances.

"Did you ever express these strong concerns directly to your sister?" Angie asked.

Arlene nodded, a deep crease appearing between her brows. "We had a few heated arguments about it. Barri had stars in her eyes whenever Trevor was around, and was always making excuses for him. She refused to listen to reason."

Several long, silent moments passed and Arlene seemed lost in troubled thoughts.

Trying a new line of inquiry, Ellie asked, "Where were you on the night Barri was killed? Do the police have all of your information to confirm your where-abouts that evening?"

Arlene stiffened almost imperceptibly at the question, though her response sounded rehearsed when she finally spoke. "I was at home here all that night. I watched a movie, chatted briefly with Barri on the phone, then went to bed. The police know all this already. As I told you earlier, I would never hurt my sister."

Though Arlene seemed cooperative overall, Angie detected guardedness in her body language and in her vague alibi. She sensed they had pushed enough questions on the woman for now.

"You've been very helpful speaking with us today," Angie said warmly, though she continued to closely study Arlene. "We appreciate you taking the time to give us some background details. Please accept our deepest condolences again for your loss."

With a polite goodbye, she and Ellie made their exit from the home, both lost in thought as they walked to the car.

Once settled inside with the doors closed, Ellie immediately turned to Angie. "It seems we finally struck a nerve regarding Trevor, and she was definitely tense and evasive about her alibi for the night of the murder."

Taking a glance back at the house, Angie started the engine. "Arlene clearly loathed Trevor. It also seems no one is able to corroborate that she was at home that night."

"Plenty of motive, too, if she thought Trevor was mistreating or manipulating her sister," Ellie mused aloud. "Killing Barri could have been her twisted way of punishing both him and her sister for not heeding her warnings about the relationship."

They continued debating the possibilities and picking apart Arlene's potential motives as green fields and dense woodlands swept by outside the car windows. Angie's mind churned with additional questions.

Could Arlene's protective anger toward her sister have gradually taken a darker, more jealous turn?

Were there deeper issues of rivalry or insecurity underlying her dislike for Trevor? More insights were needed, but this felt like an important step forward.

Early the next morning before Angie headed into the bake shop, she decided to do some online research into Arlene's background, looking for anything that might hint at a darker side hidden beneath her polished exterior.

Ellie soon joined her in browsing through Arlene's social media sites and local news archives for further information. Opening her laptop, she said, "I've only got about ten minutes to spare before I have to refresh the breakfast buffet for the guests." She looked at website after website trying to find some information on the woman.

"Look at this. Arlene was arrested a few years back for getting into a physical fight with another woman she accused of being a 'romantic rival,'" Ellie said with surprise. "Apparently, they had a shouting match that turned violent outside a local bar."

Angie nodded grimly. "That's quite an explosive temper she seems to have. It doesn't line up with the mild-mannered, soft-spoken person she tried to project when we visited her."

They also found an article praising Arlene's artistic quilting and knitting work. Like her sister, she seemed very creative and entrepreneurially-minded. But Angie wondered if, beneath that busy, industrious surface, the combination of envy and jealousy might actually be a volatile, combustible mix.

"It seems she also posts rants online about female empowerment and not being constrained by traditional gender roles or expectations," Ellie commented as she scrolled through Arlene's social media feeds. "She's really fixated on asserting her independence."

Angie tapped a pen on her notepad as she absorbed the information. "If she saw Barri's upcoming marriage to Trevor as some old-fash-ioned, conformist betrayal of her principles, that might have made her even more upset about the relationship."

The deeper they dug, the more complexities and potential cracks emerged in Arlene's presentation of herself as a loving, selfless sister. Angie knew she needed to meet with Chief Martin to discuss the new questions they had about the woman.

Late in the afternoon, she met up with the police chief on a secluded oceanside bench on Robin's Point, one of her favorite thinking spots. The steady roar of waves in the background helped settle her whirling thoughts.

Chief Martin listened, asking occasional questions, as Angie detailed all they had learned about Trevor's questionable financial practices and behaviors, as well as revealing glimpses of Arlene's hidden volatility and temper.

"You point out some promising new angles and motives for us to look at," he said once she had finished presenting the latest insights. "Arlene clearly has quite a fiery temper under her polite facade. Her strong dislike for Trevor could give her reasons to want revenge against him."

Angie nodded. "My and Ellie's instincts say we should take a closer look at Arlene's relationship with her sister, as well as tracking her movements around the estimated time of the murder."

The chief assured her they were looking into Arlene as a suspect. Angie's shoulders felt lighter leaving the windswept overlook, hoping the fog shrouding the case had started to lift.

There was still a long road ahead to expose Barri's killer, but something else worried Angie. If Arlene was the one who killed her sister, what motive could she possibly have to be stalking Courtney?

It didn't fit. It didn't fit at all.

12

It was late afternoon when Orla arrived at the Victorian house after spending several hours babysitting Libby and Gigi. The girls skipped happily ahead into the kitchen, where the aroma of baked goods filled the air.

Euclid and Circe trilled from their perch on top of the fridge.

"Mmm, something smells delicious," Orla remarked, glancing over to see Angie carefully frosting a tray of mini-cupcakes.

Angie smiled in greeting as she kissed the little girls on their heads. "Hey, you two, did you have fun with Orla today?"

"We made finger puppets and put on a show," Libby said excitedly, giving Angie a big hug.

Gigi was peering at the array of colorful cupcakes. "Can we try one, Momma?"

"You sure can. Take your pick," Angie said, handing the girls napkins. "Courtney and Rufus are going to taste test the flavors to choose their favorite for their wedding cake."

Right on cue, Courtney and Ellie entered the kitchen, followed by Jenna a few minutes later.

The little girls raced to greet them. "We're trying cupcakes," Libby told her mother with a wide grin.

"Yay! It's cake tasting day," Courtney said with a grin, swiping some frosting with her finger.

Soon they were all seated around the big table looking at the red velvet, lemon, chocolate espresso, and white chocolate raspberry cupcakes, chatting and laughing while waiting for Rufus to arrive. For a moment, the underlying tensions and mysteries of the past days seemed to lift.

As the girls finished their treats and scampered off to play in the family room, Orla turned to the sisters, her expression growing serious. "I spoke with Magill yesterday," she told them, naming the psychic mentor she trusted. "She suggested you use some protective herbs and crystals to keep you safe."

The light mood dissipated instantly. "Did she

have any advice for how to combat the stalker?" Jenna asked tensely.

Orla patted her hand. "There's no advice about how to fight the stalker. You need to stay grounded in the light and seek signs from the spirit world. And know that you have allies all around, seen and unseen."

Angie sighed. "Some days it's hard to stay grounded and positive with this looming over the family."

Hoping to provide some reassurance, Ellie spoke up. "We may have a promising new suspect to focus on - Barri's sister Arlene. Angie and I visited with her and something seems off with her and her relationship with Barri."

Quickly, Angie summarized their observations about Arlene's dislike of Trevor and how she didn't have anyone to back up her claim that she was at home all night when Barri was killed.

Ellie added, "Arlene went on and on about how wonderful and sweet Barri was, but some tiny little thing about what she was saying didn't quite ring true to me."

"I felt something similar from Arlene," Angie reported.

"She certainly sounds suspicious," Orla agreed when Ellie finished. "And jealous or angry family members can have complex motives behind what they do."

Angie hesitated before voicing her reservations. "Although it seems Arlene might be involved, the more I think about it, something doesn't fit for me."

She met Orla's thoughtful gaze. "If Arlene did kill Barri, why would she have any reason to now target Courtney? Why do that? I can't see a connection."

Orla pondered Angie's point. "It is odd ... unless perhaps the woman is lashing out at any young bride-to-be as a twisted form of vengeance."

Jenna shook her head. "I'm with Angie, that seems like a stretch." She turned to Angie and Ellie. "Did you two uncover any other promising leads?"

The sisters reminded them about Trevor's financial issues and the tensions in his relationship with Barri. Though motive existed, his grief had seemed heartbreakingly genuine.

"There are still missing pieces," Angie concluded, drumming her fingers absently on the table. "We just have to keep digging."

Orla gave a nod. "Something will turn up." She checked the time. "I need to get going. I'll let you know when we have a date and time to meet with

Magill in person. For now, stay safe all of you. Call me if you need me." The woman left the house and headed home.

Further speculation about Arlene was cut short by the kitchen backdoor swinging open. Rufus' face broke into a grin when he saw the array of small colorful cupcakes.

"Please tell me I get to sample every one of these," he kidded, snagging one frosted in pale blue and taking an appreciative bite.

The mood lightened as the small group tasted and critiqued each flavor option, weighing comparisons and combinations. Angie handed out ballots for everyone to vote anonymously on their favorites.

The taste-testing was interrupted by Mr. Finch, who had just returned from working at the candy shop, bustling into the kitchen. "My timing is lucky as always," he remarked as he sat down at the table and chose a red velvet cupcake to sample. "What did I miss?"

"We're just about to vote on our favorite," Courtney told the man. "Take your time making your decision. Here's a secret ballot for you to rank the flavors with your favorite being marked number 1."

In the end, it came down to a perfect tie between

red velvet and white chocolate raspberry. "Why choose?" Angie suggested. "We can do a tiered cake with layers of both."

The cats meowed their approval.

Rufus and Courtney loved the idea. As he pulled her close and popped the last bite of cupcake into her mouth, Courtney smiled up at him. "Two perfect flavors together, just like us."

Once the cake flavor debate was settled, Mr. Finch turned to Rufus. "Your parents are still planning to fly in next week for the festivities?"

Rufus nodded, his expression a mix of affection and amusement. "Mum and Dad don't like to stay in one place for long, but they wouldn't miss Courtney's and my special day."

He gave a wry little smile. "They're eccentric but I adore them. My mum is American. She was born in Connecticut but went to university at Oxford. They'll only stay in town for two nights. They love to travel and the day after the wedding, they're off to Africa."

Courtney leaned her head on Rufus' shoulder. "I can't wait for them to be here, even if it's only for a couple of days."

Angie's heart swelled at her sister's and almost brother-in-law's love and excitement despite the lurking troubles. She hoped that the joining of these two lives could go on without dark shadows falling over the joyous occasion.

Ellie said, "When we were talking to Orla about Arlene being a suspect, she mentioned the stalker possibly targeting any young woman who was getting married soon. Who knows about Courtney and Rufus' upcoming wedding? The people who are invited of course, but it's a small celebration." She looked at her youngest sister. "Did you place any announcements in the news?"

Courtney nodded. "Yes, remember we put an announcement of our engagement in the Sweet Cove weekly newspaper."

"Oh, right," Ellie said. "I forgot about that."

"Did Barri have an announcement posted in the news for her engagement?" Jenna asked.

Angie went to the kitchen island and tapped at her laptop searching for anything in the area news. "An engagement announcement for Barri and Trevor was placed on both the Silver Cove and Sweet Cove news outlets."

Ellie suggested, "Maybe the killer saw the stories and targeted the young women that way."

"Are there any other announcements for

upcoming weddings listed in those news outlets?" Courtney questioned.

"There's one for this coming weekend," Angie told them.

Mr. Finch looked alarmed. "We should inform Chief Martin of our suspicions. That young woman might be in danger."

Courtney asked, "What's her name?"

Angie looked back at the notice. "Leeann Paulson. The groom-to-be is Dennis Place."

Courtney sat up straight. "I know who she is. We met at a business conference in Boston about a year ago. We talked about starting a group for small businesswomen in Sweet Cove and Silver Cove, but we let it slide and didn't do anything to get it going."

"Where does she live?" Jenna asked.

"In Silver Cove." Courtney's eyes were wide. "Leeann is a ceramic artist. She owns the pottery shop on Main Street in Silver Cove. Barri was a small business owner and so am I. Could this be the connection between us?"

"Can you get in touch with Leeann?" Angie asked. "Find out if she's being targeted or stalked by someone?"

"I'll go to her shop later today. I'd rather talk in

person," Courtney said with a shrug. "It's a weird and sensitive topic of conversation."

"I'll go with you," Rufus told her.

Angie crossed her fingers that this would be an important piece of information that would finally help the puzzle take shape.

13

The Pottery Nook was located right on the main street of the pretty seaside village of Silver Cove. Large storefront windows let the afternoon sunlight stream in, highlighting the handmade pottery displayed on the white shelves. The space was warm and inviting, with wide plank wood floors and light aqua-painted walls.

Near the entrance, wooden racks held rows of glazed mugs in lively hues like coral, seafoam green, and sunny yellow bearing stamped designs like seashells, sailboats, and lighthouses. Further inside, white-washed hutches and tables displayed an array of pottery pieces like serving bowls, platters, vases, and pitchers in muted red-brown, blues, greens, and sand colors.

The back wall featured long shelves lined with unique ceramic sculptures - playful octopuses, wise owls, leaping dolphins, and sleeping cats, and nearby, a spinning rack held packs of ceramic coasters printed with vintage maritime maps. The shop had a tranquil, relaxed vibe enhanced by instrumental guitar music playing softly in the background.

A twelve-foot-long wooden counter painted robin's egg blue ran along the left side, where a coffee and tea bar had been set up for the patrons. The right side of the space had whitewashed wainscoting and shuttered windows overlooking the harbor. A few patrons sat chatting at the small tables near the windows while enjoying coffee, tea, or sparkling water.

Shelves built into nooks displayed ceramic plates and bowls ready for decorating. One night a week was paint night with bins of markers and paints to allow customers to customize their pottery pieces. Brightly decorated kites hung overhead on the ceiling, adding pops of color.

Behind a glass wall, several potters were working at their wheels.

With its relaxed seaside charm and ever-changing collections of locally crafted pottery, The

Pottery Nook was a favorite spot for tourists and townies alike, who appreciated the artistry of the shop's wares.

Courtney and Rufus walked into the shop and looked around for the owner. Leeann Paulson had light brown hair with blonde highlights, blue eyes, and was of medium height with a slender build. The young woman stood behind the checkout counter wrapping a few plates for a customer when she noticed Courtney and waved.

Once the sale was rung up and the items placed in a brown paper bag with the business' logo on it, Leeann came out from the counter and hurried over to the couple.

"Courtney! I've been thinking about you. I thought we should get together and talk about starting that group for area businesswomen."

"I'm sorry we didn't get on that right after the conference last year." Courtney introduced Rufus to the woman, and after a few minutes of pleasant chat, she lowered her voice. "I came out to ask you something kind of weird."

Leeann cocked her head a bit to the side. "What is it?"

"By any chance, have you been receiving notes or small gifts from a secret admirer?"

Leeann's eyes went wide. "How did you know?"

"Did you see the news about Barri Lewiston's death?" Courtney asked.

"I did. I knew Barri a little. I couldn't believe what happened to her ... and right on the eve of her wedding. It was just so terrible." With a worried expression, Leeann gestured to the back of the shop. "Do you want to come sit in my office so we can talk privately?"

Courtney and Rufus followed the woman to the rear of the pottery shop and into a small office with a desk and chair, two side chairs, and a shelf displaying pretty pottery pieces.

"Please, sit." Leeann took the desk chair, and the young couple settled into the side chairs. "How did you know I had a secret admirer?"

"Because I have one, too," Courtney admitted. "Barri had one as well. We're concerned that this stalker might be targeting young women business owners who are getting married soon."

Leeann blinked, pondering Courtney's statements. "You think this admirer was the one who killed Barri?" She shivered as her face seemed to pale slightly.

"We think so," Rufus told her. "How many notes or gifts have you received?"

"Three." Leeann glanced out the window for a moment, a tense look on her face.

"Can you tell us what they were?"

Leeann turned her head to face them. "One was a beaded bracelet with my name spelled out with individual beads. A short four-line poem came with it. The second time, it was a gold heart-shaped locket with a short note about how much the person admired me. The last thing I got showed up yesterday at my house. It was a tiny wooden heart that fit in the palm of my hand. There was no note that time." The young woman looked down at her hands. "I thought it was some teenager who had a crush on me, or maybe a college student who admired me from afar." Leeann looked up. "It seems this is far more than some innocent kid with a crush."

"I think so, too," Courtney admitted. "Did you keep the things? Do you still have them?"

Leeann nodded. "It felt wrong to just throw them out."

"I'd like to tell Police Chief Martin from Sweet Cove about this," Courtney informed the woman. "Would you mind if he comes out to talk to you? He might want to take the items and have them checked for evidence. I saw your engagement announcement in the news. I'm sorry to lay this on you less than a week before your wedding."

Leeann's fingers trembled a little when she brushed her bangs to the side. "Do you think I'm in danger?"

"I hate to say it, but it's possible we're both in danger." Courtney told them about the notes and gifts she'd received. "The first time the things were left at my candy shop and the second delivery was left on the porch of our house. I have to admit I was pretty freaked out the person knew where I lived."

"I'm seeing all of this in a new light ... one that freaks me out, too. I thought it was all an innocent crush; something cute. Not now." Leeann's eyes filled up. "Am I going to end up like Barri? She got killed the night before her wedding. What should I do?"

"You're not going to end up like Barri. We'll talk to Chief Martin. He knows the Silver Cove police chief. They'll figure out what should be done. They'll keep you safe."

"Should we postpone the wedding?" Leeann's lower lip quivered.

"You, your fiancé, and your family should talk about that." Courtney looked at Rufus. "We're getting married the weekend after you. We're not going to postpone."

"We don't want some crazy person dictating our lives," Rufus said with a touch of anger in his tone.

Courtney said, "I'll have Chief Martin contact you. He'll give you advice. Listen to what he and the Silver Cove police chief have to say, then talk it over with people you trust. That way, you'll be able to make the best decision for you."

"Wow, my day has not gone the way I thought it was going to go." Leeann rubbed the back of her neck.

"I'm really sorry to spring this on you," Courtney told her, "but we thought you had to know."

"I'm grateful for the warning," Leeann said. "Do you have any idea who could be doing this to us? Do the police have any idea who killed Barri?"

Courtney's shoulders slumped. "The police are working hard to find the killer, but we don't have any idea who the stalker might be. When we found out you were getting married soon, we decided to come and talk to you to see if you'd received things from a secret admirer. We've made some connections ... the three of us who have been targeted are all businesswomen living in either Sweet Cove or Silver Cove."

"And the three of you have weddings coming up soon," Rufus pointed out.

"Is it someone who frequents our stores?" Leeann questioned.

"It's possible," Courtney told her.

"Are there any other links between you three?" Rufus asked. "Do you have any of the same community connections? Mutual friends? Where you get your hair cut? Anything at all?"

Courtney and Leeann discussed what things they might have in common, but came up lacking.

"Why would someone want to kill us because we're businesswomen who are about to be married?" Leeann asked, knowing there wasn't an answer. She shook her head in despair. "I just can't wrap my mind around someone wanting to harm me simply for being a young entrepreneur about to be married. It's terrifying."

She wrapped her arms around herself as if warding off a sudden chill. "Most days I don't even think about the fact that I'm a business owner. I just do what I love - making pottery. Customers come in to chat and admire the pieces as much as to buy them."

Leeann's eyes took on a faraway look. "When Dennis proposed it felt like such a natural next step for us after being together for three years. I was over-joyed thinking about combining our lives and families. Now this twisted stalker has turned everything dark and uncertain."

Courtney nodded. "Believe me, I understand exactly how you feel. It's a happy time turned upside down."

Rufus leaned forward. "Try not to despair. Chief Martin is very skilled. He'll give you strong security advice and will work with the Silver Cove Police Department. They have a real chance to catch this monster before he can hurt anyone else."

Leeann looked slightly hopeful after his assurances. "I really hope you're right. It's just hard feeling so powerless. I always thought I was pretty independent - running my own shop, making my own choices." She frowned. "Now some stranger can upend everything."

"That won't happen," Courtney said firmly. "Everyone will be on guard."

Rufus gave a nod of agreement. "The authorities will handle surveillance and make sure you and Dennis are protected." He managed a small, encouraging smile. "Don't postpone just yet. We all deserve happy weddings full of love and fun, creepy stalkers be damned."

Leeann let out a surprised huff of laughter, the first break in the tension. "Well said. I'm not going to let a monster rob me of everything we've been happily planning for the past year."

Courtney smiled before standing up. "Chief Martin will call you soon. I'll give him your number. Rufus and I will be keeping in close touch with you. And soon this will be behind us, and will be just a bizarre, weird memory."

As they left the office, they almost bumped into one of the potters who had been working at one of the wheels.

"This is my friend Lisa. She works here part-time," Leeann told them. "Some of her pottery is on sale in the shop."

Lisa shook hands with them and smiled. "Nice to meet you."

Courtney felt a sharp zip of something when she held Lisa's hand, but wasn't sure what it was and quickly dismissed it.

At the shop door, the three exchanged hugs and said goodbye, and as Rufus and Courtney stepped out into the sunshine, they shared a hopeful look.

"Thank heavens we were able to warn Leeann," Courtney said.

Rufus took her hand in his. "As Mr. Finch says, 'forewarned is forearmed.'"

14

With Euclid and Circe trotting ahead of them, Jenna and Angie walked through the family room to Mr. Finch's first-floor apartment. Angie's palms were slick with nervous sweat, and ever since Jenna's and Libby's visions of the ghostly woman warning of impending danger, Angie's nerves had been on edge. She hoped Mr. Finch's latest sketches might give them some insight.

Warm light spilled from the open door of the cozy apartment. As the scent of oil paints tickled Angie's nose, Mr. Finch's deep voice called out, "Come in, come in."

The older man was arranging framed canvases along the walls. He beamed at the sisters, his eyes twinkling behind his spectacles. "I have the sketch-book ready to show you when you're ready to look."

Mr. Finch had changed some of the art hanging on the living room walls, where seascapes depicting frothy waves and a weathered lighthouse were now displayed. On another wall, Mr. Finch had captured the beauty and grace of the Victorian mansion with its peaked towers rising against a bright blue sky.

Angie's eyes were drawn to a grouping of whimsical pencil sketches on the far wall - portraits of the mansion's resident cats. Circe sprawled lazily across a windowsill, while a sly-looking Euclid peered around a corner, his green eyes glinting.

"These are wonderful," Jenna said warmly as she admired the artwork. "You perfectly captured the cats' personalities."

"Why, thank you, my dear," Mr. Finch said, pleased. He stroked his chin thoughtfully. "I must admit, lately I've been attempting something a bit different with my drawings. I'm trying to capture more than just the surface image and trying to show a deeper essence, you might say."

He gestured to the sketch of Euclid. "Our mysterious feline companion here has many layers to his grand personality."

Mr. Finch turned to Angie. "Are you and Miss Jenna ready to look at my sketchbook?"

Angie wrung her hands nervously. Her fear of finding ominous visions in Mr. Finch's artwork filled her veins, but she wanted to help shed light on the danger threatening those she loved.

Steeling herself, Angie sat down at the table next to her twin sister, and Mr. Finch angled the sketches so both sisters could see them at the same time while he slowly turned the pages.

In a few moments, the room seemed to fall away as Angie narrowed her gaze on Euclid's glowing green eyes. A familiar dizziness swept over her ... then flashes of hazy scenes began to materialize.

She saw a formless gray void, and then outlines of a living room took shape. A slender blonde woman in a blue dress stood with her back turned. As Angie watched, the woman slowly rotated to face forward. Her lovely features contorted into a silent shriek, hands clawing the air in terror.

When that vision melted away, Angie found herself peering into the murky interior of a pottery studio. Shelves lined the shadowy walls, crowded with precariously stacked bowls and vases.

At a worktable beneath a halo of lamplight, a young woman with long hair bent intently over a spinning pottery wheel. Her hands were coated in wet clay as she shaped a delicate vessel. When Angie watched, the young woman lifted her head, revealing a pleading look in her wide, frightened eyes. Her mouth opened in a silent wail before the scene faded into blackness.

The inky void swirled again and Angie now stood in a darkened bedroom viewing a figure sprawled on the floor, her slender shoulders shaking with sobs. Stepping nearer, Angie saw it was Courtney, her face buried in her hands. Her younger sister lifted her head, cheeks stained with tears, and looked directly at Angie with agonized eyes. Her pale face contorted as she let out an earsplitting scream.

Angie reeled, clapping her hands over her ears. Courtney's tormented face still swam before her eyes. She had to stop this somehow.

Just then the vision changed once more, and this time, Angie froze as she looked down at a figure on the cement floor of a dark room. Lying broken and battered in the gleam of a flashlight was a young man.

"No!" Angie cried out as she staggered closer on rubbery legs. The young man's half-lidded eyes stared vacantly upward. Blood oozed from a gash on his head. "Rufus!"

At the sound of Angie's voice, Rufus' eyes shifted weakly to meet hers. Blood trickled from his parted lips as he croaked, "Help ... me..." His hand twitched toward Angie before going limp.

Rushing forward, she screamed hoarsely, but Rufus and the dark room were already dissolving. The visions released their hold, receding like the tide as Angie found herself gazing once more into Euclid's glowing eyes in the sketchbook.

Gasping, Angie's head snapped back as Mr. Finch's living room swam into focus.

"Angie," Jenna cried in alarm, catching her sister's shoulders. "What happened? What did you see?"

The cats rushed to Angie's side while Mr. Finch hovered next to her, his brow creased anxiously beneath his white hair. "My dear, are you all right? You experienced a vision?"

"The visions." Angie choked out between heaving breaths. "They were horrible." Her body swayed in the chair and Jenna helped hold her steady.

"Just sit for a minute. Take deep breaths," Jenna soothed, squeezing Angie's trembling hand. She shot Mr. Finch a worried look.

"Let me fetch you a glass of water, dear," Mr. Finch said gently. He disappeared into the kitchen, returning a moment later with a tall glass.

Angie accepted it with quivering hands. The icy water helped ground her as the disturbing visions continued to flash through her mind. She took a steadying breath and haltingly described what she had witnessed.

Jenna and Mr. Finch exchanged grave looks as Angie recounted the terrifying scenes.

"They felt like they were real," Angie whispered, a chill running down her spine. "The first image was of Barri, and the second was of Leeann. The last two showed Courtney and Rufus. We have to protect them."

Mr. Finch slowly ran a hand down his wrinkled face. "I fear you may be right. My drawings acted as a conduit and allowed you to glimpse events in the past and those yet to come."

"The future can be changed," Jenna said. "When I saw those images of Angie in a coffin several years ago, it didn't come true. We can stop terrible things from happening."

Mr. Finch exhaled heavily. "We will fight for the future we want."

Angie's heart still raced. After all this time, after

overcoming so much adversity together, was their extraordinary luck about to run out? Would they be powerless to prevent the killer from striking again?

Mr. Finch seemed to read her gloomy thoughts. "We will hold tight to hope, Miss Angie," he said encouragingly, giving her shoulder a paternal pat. "Your visions have granted us a glimpse of what may be. That knowledge can help us change the course of events, even small differences may be enough."

Angie nodded, clinging to the ray of hope. They had to try. She rose on still-wobbly legs, her jaw set with resolve.

"Come on, let's go find Miss Courtney and Rufus," Mr. Finch said. "They must be told what you saw without delay."

The three hurried from the apartment with the cats trailing after them.

Perhaps it was already too late to alter the course that had been set in motion, but Angie and the others would set their minds to protecting those they loved. They had done it before. It was possible to keep bad things from happening.

The family members gathered around the kitchen table to discuss Angie's vision, and the cats jumped up to the top of the fridge to listen. Full of nervous energy, Angie couldn't sit still and was standing at the kitchen island baking some traditional scones while still taking part in the conversation.

"Visions don't necessarily predict the future," Rufus said after initially being upset about what Angie had seen. "The images warn of danger, but we can fight it."

"Could you see where we were in the vision?" Courtney asked her sister. "Were there any clues about the space we were in?"

Angie stopped mixing the batter and looked off across the room trying to remember. "I'm not sure. It was so dark and everything was shrouded in a heavy fog."

"Could you tell what we were wearing?" Courtney questioned.

With her eyes wide, Angie looked at her youngest sister. "Yes, I did see what you had on. You were wearing black slacks and your pink dressy shirt with the ruffle down the front." She turned to Rufus. "You had on dark slacks and a pale blue buttoned-down shirt."

Rufus asked, "So if we never wear those items, does that mean bad things won't happen to us?"

Mr. Finch looked doubtful. "I don't think wearing other pieces of clothing will make a difference."

Ellie looked around the room. "Where's Jenna?"

Angie sighed. "She wanted a few minutes to think. She went to her studio."

"Should I check on her?" Ellie wore a worried expression.

"No, she'll be okay." Angie cut rounds from the batter and placed them on the baking sheet before slipping it into the oven. "She'll join us in a few minutes."

Courtney glanced about looking anxious. "I just can't believe someone wants to hurt Rufus and me. Who would do such an awful thing?"

Rufus wrapped an arm around her, giving her a reassuring squeeze. "We'll be okay."

Ellie shook her head in disgust at the mess of it all. "Angie's vision was crystal clear. Someone means you and Rufus harm, but I believe you'll get through this in one piece and the stalker will be caught."

Rufus' mouth set in a firm line. "Well, they'll have to go through me first if they want to get anywhere near Courtney."

Mr. Finch nodded approvingly. "We'll all be keeping a close eye out and will be ready for whatever comes."

"I hate to say this, but do you think we should consider postponing the wedding?" Courtney asked her fiancé in a small voice. "I don't want anything to happen to you."

Rufus took Courtney's hands, gazing into her eyes. "This is just a bump in the road." He smiled encouragingly. "Nothing and no one will stop us from being together."

"Chief Martin and his team will keep us safe," Mr. Finch said gently.

Angie came over to the table, wiping her hands on a dish towel. "Mr. Finch is right. We can take precautions and security will be tight, and if you two are sure you want to go forward, we'll go ahead with the wedding as planned."

Courtney managed a small smile and took a deep, steadying breath. "Okay then, we stay the course ... for now."

Jenna walked into the room and poured herself a cup of coffee. "What did I miss?"

The group provided a recap of the discussion.

"I agree with going ahead with the wedding if

that's what Courtney and Rufus want to do." Jenna sat at the long table next to Mr. Finch.

"Are you all right, Miss Jenna?" Mr. Finch inquired.

"Sometimes, I find the visions Angie has upsetting. I just needed a few minutes by myself." Wrapping her hands around her mug, she added, "That was only part of the reason I wanted to be alone. I went to my studio to try to summon Nana. I hoped she'd materialize and give us some advice, but nothing happened. I want to be able to help and seeing ghosts is my way to do that, but I need the ghosts to cooperate and so far, they haven't."

"Keep trying," Courtney encouraged with a smile. "You know how finicky ghosts can be."

The comment brought a smile to Jenna's face. "I sure do."

The oven timer dinged and Ellie almost jumped out of her seat causing everyone to chuckle.

"My jittery nerves can't take much more of this," Ellie said wryly.

On her way to the oven, Angie said, "Hopefully we'll get more clues soon about who's behind these threats. We'll figure it out."

The cats trilled from their refrigerator perch.

When Angie removed the scones from the oven,

their pleasant aroma filled the kitchen. "Come on, let's eat. We all know sweets fix everything," she told the others with a grin as she set raspberry jam on the table.

Ellie went to get the bowl of whipped cream from the fridge, Rufus poured coffee and tea, Courtney took down dessert plates from the cabinet, Mr. Finch lit the candles, and Angie arranged the scones on a platter, and then they all sat together at the table to enjoy.

15

The morning sun filtered through the trees, dappling the winding country road in shadows as Angie drove her SUV toward Silver Cove. Courtney fidgeted in the passenger seat beside her.

"Do you think Barri's brother can give us some insights?" Courtney asked, breaking the pensive silence.

Angie kept her eyes on the road. "Joseph Lewiston might know things that could be useful. He lived in the same town and interacted with the townspeople."

Courtney nodded, though she looked uncertain. Angie didn't blame her. Interviewing Barri's brother was a long shot, but they needed to follow every lead.

Ten minutes later, Angie pulled up to a modest Cape Cod-style house nestled on a wooded lot. They had an appointment to speak with the man, who had recently returned from a trip to London.

The front door swung open before they could knock, revealing a tall, slender man with shaggy dark blond hair. Dressed in jeans and a wrinkled t-shirt, he regarded them with sharp blue eyes.

"You must be the sisters Chief Martin told me about," he said. "Come on in."

The living room was cluttered with camera equipment and unframed photographs. Joseph waved for them to sit on a modern-style sofa.

"So, you're investigating my sister's murder," he said without preamble, dropping into an armchair. "Seems like the police have everything under control, if you ask me."

Angie bristled at his dismissive tone. "As Chief Martin probably told you, we're consulting for the police trying to gain additional insights that might help lead to the killer."

Joseph snorted. "Well, I won't be much use."

"Were you informed about Barri's death when you were in London?" Angie asked.

"Yeah, but I couldn't get back any sooner than I did. I had a contract to do fashion shoots and had to honor the contract, and what difference would it have made anyway? Barri was already dead."

Courtney said, "That's too bad you couldn't get back home sooner. I guess your parents might have appreciated your support."

Joseph said, "It wouldn't have mattered. My parents are fully self-sufficient. They don't need me around."

Courtney leaned forward. "We'd still appreciate anything you could share. What was your relationship with your sister like?"

Joseph stretched his long legs out in front of him. "There were seven years between us. We were too far apart in age to be close. Barri was the baby of the family." He shrugged. "By the time she was a teenager, I was already out of the house traveling the world. Barri and I didn't exactly see eye to eye. She wanted a regular job. She wanted a family. Financial security was important to her. I honestly didn't feel much about Barri's death – sure it was horrible she was murdered, but we really didn't have much of a relationship."

"So you didn't keep in touch with her on a regular basis?" Angie asked.

"Nah. We both had our own orbits. We lived

separate lives. We didn't interact much. We didn't really know each other very well."

Angie and Courtney exchanged a look. Clearly there was no love lost between the siblings.

"What can you tell us about your parents?" Angie questioned.

Joseph smirked. "You haven't met them? My folks are free-spirited people. They raised me and my sisters in a very Bohemian way. I learned from them to be myself and to follow my interests no matter if they were out of the ordinary." He stood abruptly, striding over to rummage through a box on the cluttered counter. "Let me paint you a picture," he said, handing them a faded Polaroid snapshot. "This is a photo of my parents when they were young."

It showed a teenage Joseph with two smiling adults - a willowy woman in an embroidered peasant dress with a flower garland in her flowing blonde hair, and a bearded man in ripped jeans playing a guitar.

Courtney studied the photo. "They seem ..."

"Unconventional?" Joseph supplied the adjective. "That's putting it mildly. My parents encouraged me to follow my own path, blaze my own trail through life."

He dropped back into his chair. "After high

school, I took off to travel the world with my camera. I never looked back."

Angie's eyes roamed over the artistic black and white photographs adorning the walls ... images of street markets in Marrakesh, misty Scottish highlands, rice paddies in Vietnam.

"Your photography work is quite good," she said politely.

Joseph shrugged. "It pays the bills."

"Do you get along with your parents?" Courtney asked.

"Well enough. We didn't see each other much once I moved out." Joseph leaned back, lacing his fingers behind his head. "But I knew Barri stayed close with them. She was always the dutiful one."

Angie asked, "Are you married?"

Joseph said, "No, I've never been married. It's not my thing."

"Do you have a partner?" Courtney questioned.

"I never had time for someone else."

Courtney asked, "Do you have any kids?"

Joseph shook his head. "I never wanted a family. It would tie me down too much. I wanted to be free to do what I want; pursue my art."

Angie decided to change tacks. "What can you tell us about Trevor Ralston, Barri's fiancé?"

Joseph's lip curled derisively. "That clown? He's always flashing his cash, trying to impress everyone. He's a fool with money; a complete fool." He snickered. "Trevor is superficial and loves flashy things – it makes him feel good about himself because there's nothing worthwhile about the guy. But it was all a front – the guy is drowning in debt. I don't know why Barri was with him."

Courtney stared at the man.

"Did Barri know about his money problems?" Angie questioned.

"Who knows?" Joseph stood again, pacing over to peer out the window with his back to them. "I think she liked the glitzy show he put on. I don't think she ever realized it was all a sham. You'll have to ask my parents. They might know if Barri knew about Trevor's troubles."

"When did you leave for London?" Angie questioned.

"I took a late flight out of Boston the night before my sister's body was discovered."

He turned, regarding Angie and Courtney coolly. "I know what you're both thinking. Maybe I fought with my sister, killed her in a fit of rage, then headed for the airport. I suppose that makes me a suspect since I could have killed my sister and still made it to Boston on time. But what would be my reason? What's my motive? There isn't one."

Angie opened her mouth to protest, but Joseph barreled on. "Do I have an alibi? Not really. I worked all day in my studio, packed for the trip after dinner, and then took a ride share to the airport in Boston. I was in London doing fashion shoots the whole week before I came home."

He crossed his arms. "I didn't have time to fight with Barri. I was busy that day. So unless you think I teleported myself across town and back again, you can cross me off your suspect list."

Angie held his challenging gaze evenly. "We're just trying to understand the full picture. Your perspective on the family dynamic is helpful."

Joseph's tense posture relaxed slightly. He glanced at his watch. "Look, I need to head out for a shoot. But one thing you should know..." He met their eyes solemnly. "Barri was too good for this world. She deserved better than what she got."

With that, he showed them out. Angie's mind spun as they walked to the car. Joseph's defensiveness might signal he was hiding something, but what?

"He's definitely not brother of the year,"

Courtney said as she buckled her seatbelt. "Do you think he could've killed Barri?"

"He could have. I don't know." Angie turned the ignition. "What did you sense about him?"

"Besides being self-involved and sort of judgmental, I'm not sure about him. I didn't like him, but was that me sensing he'd done something terrible or that I didn't care for him as a person? For now, he stays on my suspect list."

As she navigated the winding roads back to Sweet Cove, Angie's thoughts kept returning to Joseph's apparent indifference toward his sister. Indifference didn't mean he was a killer.

Back at the Victorian, Angie headed straight for the kitchen since baking always helped clear her mind. Soon she was whisking up batter for snickerdoodle cupcakes, trying to infuse the mixture with calming energy.

As the kitchen filled with the sweet aroma of cinnamon, Angie's tense shoulders relaxed. The others would be gathering soon to discuss their next steps, but for now, she allowed herself a moment of calm.

Right on cue, Ellie and Jenna wandered in, followed by Mr. Finch with a purring Circe curled in his arms.

"Mm, something smells divine," Mr. Finch declared, taking an appreciative whiff.

Ellie grinned at her sister. "Let me guess – snickerdoodle cupcakes?"

Angie smiled, removing a tray of perfect golden cupcakes. "As soon as I frost them, you can help yourselves."

As Ellie, Jenna, and Mr. Finch enjoyed the treats, Angie recounted the visit with Joseph Lewiston.

Mr. Finch's bushy brows drew together. "The young man seems rather detached from the family," he remarked. "I wonder..."

He was interrupted by hurried footsteps, then Courtney burst into the kitchen looking upset. Rufus was on her heels, his face grim.

Angie straightened in alarm. "What's wrong?"

"I just heard from Leeann," Courtney said shakily. "She got another gift and note from her stalker last night."

Shocked exclamations filled the kitchen.

"What did the note say?" Jenna asked.

Rufus shook his head, his jaw tight. "Just more cryptic ramblings about Leeann being 'his soulmate.' But the gifts are escalating - this one was a necklace with a small diamond."

"This is an unstable person trying to force a connection," Mr. Finch said gravely.

Ellie shuddered. "Poor Leeann must be terrified. Her wedding is in days."

Angie stayed quiet, her stomach in knots. Between her ominous visions and Leeann being actively stalked, time was running out to stop the threat looming over them.

Rufus voiced her thoughts. "We need to catch this guy before he hurts someone else." He paced the kitchen like a caged tiger.

"There must be some link between the victims we're missing," Jenna said.

"The man may have visited the women's shops and was drawn to them," Mr. Finch guessed. "Barri, Leeann, and Courtney are very similar physically."

Ellie asked, "Can you try looking in Mr. Finch's sketches again for any clues?"

Angie swallowed hard, thinking back to the chilling visions she'd just had. "I can try again."

Mr. Finch gave her shoulder an encouraging pat. "No need to rush, my dear. When the time is right, look at the artwork again, but only if you feel able."

She nodded, grateful for his understanding. Anxious to shift focus back to the investigation,

Angie relayed some of the highlights from their talk with Joseph.

"He seems completely indifferent about Barri. He said he really didn't feel anything about her death," she told them. "And he mentioned Trevor is deep in debt despite appearances."

Ellie tapped her chin thoughtfully. "Could that be a motive? Maybe Joseph felt excluded by Barri. Maybe he tried to be a brother to her, and she rebuffed him."

"He'll stay on the suspect list for now," Angie said wishing they could catch a break with the case. She knew they were grasping at straws, and clues were slipping through their fingers.

16

The late afternoon sun shined down on Angie and Courtney as they made their way up the stone walkway leading to a sprawling farmhouse. Vibrant flower gardens bursting with color bordered the path, and wind chimes tinkled in the gentle breeze.

They had come to the home to interview Ross and Penny Flynn-Lewiston, the grieving parents of murder victim Barri Lewiston. Hopefully, the couple could provide insights into their daughter's life and relationships that might shed light on the ongoing investigation.

Courtney rang the bell and a moment later the carved oak door swung open. A slender woman in her sixties with shoulder-length hair regarded them with kind eyes.

"You must be Angie and Courtney," she said in a musical voice. "Chief Martin told us you'd be coming today. Please, come in."

The woman, Penny Flynn-Lewiston, led them into a homey living room decorated with comfortable overstuffed furniture and colorful artwork. Her movements were graceful and light-footed and made Angie think the woman might have been a dancer.

A powerfully built man with gray hair rose from an armchair to greet them. His eyes were somber, but his smile was welcoming. "I'm Ross, Barri's father," he said, shaking their hands. "Thank you for coming."

Angie and Courtney offered their condolences. Though grief flickered across the couple's faces, an aura of contentment surrounded them.

Penny gestured for the sisters to sit. "Can I get you some tea? Water?"

Soon they were settled on the sofa, teacups in hand, as Penny sank onto a chair nearby. Ross stood gazing out the bay window with his hands clasped behind his back.

"We appreciate you taking the time to speak with us," Angie began gently. "We're trying to learn as much as we can about Barri and the people in her life. Anything you can share will be helpful."

Penny smiled sadly. "Barri was sunshine personified, so talented, so caring and warm. I still can't believe she's gone. I expect her to walk through the backdoor any minute."

Ross turned from the window and took a seat next to his wife, his craggy face pensive. "She was the baby of the family. We doted on her even more after..." His voice grew hoarse.

Penny reached out and took her husband's hand. "After our daughter Amy passed away," she finished softly.

Courtney's eyes widened in surprise. The Lewistons had lost two daughters?

Sensing the question, Ross said heavily, "Amy died of leukemia when she was eight. Barri was only a toddler then. We were overprotective of her after that."

He managed a wistful smile. "Not that Barri needed protecting. She was the most positive child imaginable. She found joy in the simplest things."

Penny nodded, dabbing at her eyes with a tissue. "Oh, how she loved creating things, designing new pieces, working with the fabric ... it made her so happy."

Angie hoped easing into lighter topics might put the couple more at ease. "I understand you have amazing gardens here. Barri must have enjoyed spending time outdoors."

"Oh, yes." Penny's face lit up. "Let me give you a tour."

Soon they were strolling through the rambling gardens surrounding the farmhouse. Penny pointed out the varieties of roses, iris, peonies, and hydrangeas she nurtured. Angie could envision a young Barri playing hide-and-seek among the lush flowers.

Back in the house, Penny offered them more tea and homemade sugar cookies. Angie took the opening to gently turn the conversation toward Barri's siblings.

"We spoke recently with your son Joseph," she began. "He seems to have a unique perspective on family life."

Ross harrumphed, settling back into his armchair. "That's one way to put it. Joseph has always been something of a rebel."

Penny gave her husband a knowing look. "What Ross means is that Joseph is very independent. Free-spirited like us, but more self-focused." She shrugged. "He and his sisters didn't have much in common. Joseph has always followed his own path."

Angie recalled Joseph's apparent indifference

toward his sister's murder. "Did that bother Barri, being disconnected from her brother?"

"At times." Penny's brow furrowed. "But they were so far apart in age. Barri learned to accept that Joseph preferred solitude and adventure to family ties."

Ross leaned forward, his eyes troubled. "To be frank, we worry about Joseph. Cutting himself off from loved ones, avoiding commitment. No man is an island. It isn't a healthy way to live."

Penny looked kindly at her husband and then turned back to Angie and Courtney. "Barri tried reaching out to Joseph over the years, but he often rebuffed her efforts. I know that hurt her."

Angie nodded. "What can you tell us about your other daughter Arlene?"

Ross smiled wistfully. "Now there's a lovely girl. Arlene has a beautiful singing voice. She must have inherited it from me," he kidded giving Penny a playful wink, and she laughed. "Oh, stop."

Growing serious, Penny said, "Arlene works very hard at her paralegal job. She's quite bright and capable, but I do wish she hadn't given up performing music."

"We wanted our children to feel free to pursue their interests," Ross added a touch defensively.

"But you can't force a bird to sing if it doesn't want to."

Penny explained, "Ross is a musician who plays in different bands and works as a studio musician – he also paints. I'm an artist, sculptor, and I translate academic articles into German and French. We try to live minimally and we save and invest. We encouraged our children to live the same way. It isn't necessary to chase after riches; just live within your means, save for the future, and invest carefully."

Penny continued, "We're proud that Joseph followed his dream of being a photographer and can make a living at it, but he made us sad that he didn't try to know and appreciate his sisters."

Ross said, "Arlene is more conventional than others in the family. She prefers an office job – she works as a legal assistant. She had a lovely voice and we encouraged her to sing with my band and to seek a career in music as a vocalist, but Arlene was afraid of rejection and financial instability. She doesn't take care of her health – she sits too much, but she does work in her gardens."

Penny said, "Arlene was a bit jealous of Barri. Barri got along with everyone, had a sunny personality, and was optimistic and positive whereas Arlene is cautious, less outgoing, and self-conscious. Just two different personalities."

Angie changed course again, bringing up the touchy subject of Barri's fiancé. "We spoke with Trevor Ralston. What did you think of him?"

Ross scowled, his knuckles whitening as he clenched a fist. Penny gave him a warning look.

"Trevor concerned us," she said carefully. "His lavish spending habits were worrisome, given Barri's more prudent nature."

Ross huffed. "That boy was drowning in debt. He would have dragged Barri down with him. Barri would have had to deal with his debts. If she married Trevor, she would never have been financially stable."

Penny placed a calming hand on her husband's arm before continuing. "Trevor wasn't a good match for Barri, but she was so enchanted by his extravagant lifestyle. She thought he was making lots of money because of the way he spent it."

"Did Barri know about Trevor's financial issues?" Angie asked.

Penny hesitated. With a sidelong look at Ross, she said, "Barri knew and she was quite upset about it. She confided in me that she was having second thoughts about the marriage."

Ross stiffened, staring at his wife. "She was? Why didn't you tell me?"

"I'm sorry, dear. I wish I could have told you, but Barri asked me to keep it private. She was still thinking through what to do." Penny turned back to Angie and Courtney. "She didn't want us to influence her choice. She was afraid to call it off. She didn't want to hurt Trevor and she was afraid to disappoint everyone. I probably shouldn't speak for Barri, but personally, I believe she was on the verge of calling off the wedding."

Stunned, Angie sat back against the cushions. This was a major revelation. If Barri had decided to break the engagement, it provided Trevor with an explosive motive for murder.

Ross rubbed a hand over his stubbled chin, looking troubled. "Trevor wouldn't have taken rejection well. He had a nasty temper under that slick facade."

Penny nodded grimly. She clasped her hands in her lap, blinking back tears. "Our only comfort is knowing Barri was spared committing to the wrong man. Though we'd give anything to have her back with us."

Angie's heart ached for these loving parents. She wished the interview had yielded definitive clues, but the insight into family dynamics and relationships was certainly helpful.

After warmly thanking the couple, Angie and Courtney made their way back down the garden path, minds spinning.

"Between Joseph's indifference and Trevor's potential motive, we've got some solid threads to follow up on," Courtney said as they climbed into the car.

"Agreed. Did you pick up vibes that Ross and Penny were being fully open with us?"

Courtney nodded firmly. "They genuinely want to find Barri's killer. I'm sure of it."

"Then we keep digging." Angie's hands tightened on the steering wheel as they drove away from the rambling farmhouse.

"Suppose Trevor killed Barri," Courtney speculated. "Then why would he stalk Leeann and me?"

With a frown, Angie replied, "Good question."

Back at the Victorian, Angie headed straight for her favorite thinking spot - the kitchen. She found comfort in the familiar motions of measuring flour and cracking eggs into a mixing bowl. A batch of cinnamon cupcakes would hit the spot after the emotional interview.

Soon the rich, spicy aroma of cinnamon perfumed the air, and Angie was removing the last golden cupcakes from the oven when Ellie and Jenna stepped into the kitchen, followed by Mr. Finch.

"Ooh, cinnamon cupcakes," Ellie said, eyeing the treats appreciatively.

Angie smiled. "Go ahead, dig in. I was about to make some tea."

Soon they were all gathered around the kitchen table sampling the cupcakes as Angie recounted her conversation with Barri's parents.

"They seem like nice people," Mr. Finch remarked, brushing crumbs from his shirt.

"And it sounds like they clearly cared deeply for Barri," Jenna added. She took a thoughtful sip of tea. "Do you really think Trevor could have killed her?"

"Learning she might be about to end the engagement gives him a strong motive," Angie pointed out, "and we know he was struggling financially. Joining Barri in marriage would have given him access to her assets, which would have been a lifeline for him."

Ellie shuddered. "Ugh, maybe he loved her, but

how awful to think he might marry just to maintain his flashy facade."

Mr. Finch looked grave. "A dishonest man with his back against the wall is capable of anything."

Angie felt they were finally making headway in the investigation, but the killer was still at large, and time was running short to prevent more tragedy.

Jenna seemed to read her mind. "Have you thought any more about looking at Mr. Finch's artwork again for clues? We could really use some clear guidance right now."

Angie didn't answer right away. The disturbing visions from her last attempt still haunted her, but if it helped them stop the killer...

She met Jenna's hopeful eyes and nodded firmly. "You're right. I think I'm ready to try again."

Mr. Finch gave her shoulder an encouraging pat. "Only if you feel up to it, my dear. And we will be right by your side."

Angie mustered a brave smile.

After enjoying their tea and cupcakes, the group adjourned to Mr. Finch's cozy apartment. The cats trailed behind, as if sensing their comforting presence might be needed.

At Mr. Finch's easel sat an unfinished seascape depicting a lighthouse being buffeted by crashing gray waves. Angie studied the picture, taking steadying breaths. She could do this.

Settling onto a stool, Angie fixed her gaze on the intricate swirls of paint forming the churning ocean. Slowly, the world around her receded . . . she felt herself falling into the fathomless depths of the painting.

When foggy shapes emerged from the murky canvas waters, Angie's pulse quickened. The haze solidified into the form of a woman - Leeann, the terrified bride-to-be.

The young woman's haunted eyes begged Angie for help. Her mouth opened in a desperate scream as she appeared to run in place, unable to flee some unseen threat. Frantically, Angie grasped at the air, trying to hold onto the vision, but the inky waters swallowed it, leaving her alone in darkness.

With a gasp, Angie surfaced back in the bright apartment as the concerned faces of her family swam into focus around her.

Mr. Finch gripped Angie's shoulder, steadying her trembling body. "Welcome back, Miss Angie. We're right here with you. Just breathe."

On wobbly legs, Angie moved to an armchair. Jenna draped a soft blanket around her shoulders while Ellie pressed a glass of water into her shaking hands. The cats nuzzled against her ankles.

Once she felt calmer, Angie described the new vision. Her family members wore matching looks of concern.

Courtney came into the room. "There you are. I was looking for you." She noticed the expression of Angie's face. "Did you look into Mr. Finch's painting?"

"I did." Angie's voice was soft and weak as she described what she had seen.

"I'm not surprised." Courtney sighed. "Leeann and Dennis have postponed their wedding. Leeann was too afraid to go through with it. They want to be able to enjoy their day without looking over their shoulders the entire time."

Euclid let out a loud angry hiss as everyone stared at the youngest Roseland with worried eyes.

"And no, Rufus and I are not postponing," Courtney told them firmly. "We're going to be together."

17

Soft afternoon light filtered through the windows of Ellie's bedroom suite, as the young woman helped Courtney into her wedding gown. The polished wooden floor was draped with a white sheet to protect the delicate ivory fabric as the sisters prepared for the final fitting.

"Oh, Courtney, you look absolutely stunning," Ellie exclaimed, stepping back to admire her younger sister in the exquisite dress.

Courtney turned this way and that before the full length mirror, the gown's full skirt swishing around her. "It's magical. I never imagined such a beautiful dress," she breathed, running her hands gently over the intricate lace bodice and sleeves.

Ellie felt a rush of pride in her work. As a

talented seamstress, she had poured her heart into crafting Courtney's wedding dress. It had taken months to finish, and now, seeing her radiant sister before her, the result was worth far more than the effort.

The fitted lace bodice showcased Courtney's graceful neck and shoulders, while crystallized floral appliques caught the light. Elegant pearl buttons lined the back, ending in a small train edged with more lace. Courtney looked every inch the fairytale bride.

"The top is perfectly fitted," Courtney remarked, studying her reflection. "I don't know how you made it fit so well in all the right places."

Ellie laughed, picking up a box of pins from her worktable. "That's my little secret. Now come here and let me see if any final alterations are needed."

For the next half hour, Ellie carefully inspected every inch of the gown, making tiny adjustments. She wanted the dress to fit Courtney flawlessly for her special day.

As Ellie worked, Courtney chatted happily about the upcoming wedding. "Less than two weeks to go. I can hardly wait to walk down that aisle toward Rufus." She smiled softly. "This dress makes it feel so real. I'm going to marry the man I love."

Pins between her lips, Ellie nodded. She felt grateful that Courtney had found such a loving partner in Rufus.

Courtney twirled again, watching the skirt float around her legs. "I can just picture Rufus' expression when he sees me in this gorgeous gown."

"He's going to be spellbound," Ellie said. She fluffed the gown's layer of tulle and lace peeking out beneath the skirt's hem. "This dress design was made for you. You both deserve a beautiful day."

Her sister's blue eyes suddenly shimmered with tears. "I wish Mom could be here," Courtney said thickly.

Ellie felt a pang, glancing over at the framed photo on her dresser showing the four sisters as young girls with their mother.

"She is here," Ellie said softly, placing a hand over her heart. "Her love lives on in all of us."

Courtney clutched Ellie's hand tightly. "Oh, Ellie, that's just what it feels like." She gazed earnestly into her sister's face. "Being here with you, preparing for my wedding, it's like Mom's spirit is all around us."

Ellie nodded, her own eyes growing misty. "I feel it, too. Her warm, comforting presence." She, Courtney, Angie, and Jenna had always felt a special bond with their mother Elizabeth's kind spirit.

"Mom would be so proud of the woman you've become," Ellie continued. "So talented and strong, fully embracing all your gifts and skills."

Courtney blushed at the praise. "We're all embracing our talents more, including you." She gave Ellie a knowing look. "Your psychic senses seem to be deepening lately. I can tell you're tapping into a greater power."

Now it was Ellie's turn to blush. She busied herself tidying the pins and fabrics on her work-table. "I do feel stronger since deciding to accept my abilities," she admitted. "It happened so gradually, but I think my skills are still growing."

"It's incredible." Courtney's eyes shone with admiration. "You and Mom both have the same gift for sensing threats to those you love and deflecting the danger. You're her legacy, Ellie."

Ellie's heart swelled. She gave Courtney a teary smile. "Let's just say I have big shoes to fill when it comes to protecting this family."

Courtney laughed. "With you on the job, we're in good hands." Her expression grew somber. "Especially with this stalker still targeting brides-to-be."

Ellie set down her pincushion. "Well, I can promise you that no one is interrupting your walk down the aisle. You and Rufus deserve a wedding day free of shadows."

"With my avenging sister overseeing security," Courtney quipped, "what could go wrong?"

The two exchanged smiles. Their playful camaraderie faded as they both sensed their mother's loving presence wrapping around them like a warm embrace.

"Let's add some wedding accessories to complete your look," Ellie suggested brightly, eager to recapture the joyful mood.

She brought over an ornate jewelry box. Nestled inside was a delicate pearl necklace that had belonged to their grandmother. Ellie tenderly fastened it around Courtney's neck.

"Perfect," she declared, squeezing Courtney's shoulders and meeting her gaze in the mirror. "Something old, something new, something borrowed, something blue."

Courtney touched the necklace. "I wish Nana was here to see this."

"She'd be so pleased her necklace is being worn by such a beautiful bride," Ellie said. She picked up an antique silver hair comb with sapphire accents. "And this can be your something blue," she pronounced, fixing it in Courtney's cascade of golden curls.

Courtney turned her head this way and that, admiring the regal effect. "You've made me feel just like royalty in this gown."

On impulse, Ellie brought over the lace veil from her own wedding to let Courtney try on. The delicate tulle floated over her shining hair and shoulders like a cloud.

"Wow." Courtney blinked back more happy tears. "Now I really look like a bride."

The sisters hugged tightly. Ellie felt certain their mother was right there with them, sharing in the moment between her girls.

"I wish I could freeze this feeling forever," Courtney whispered. She then straightened her shoulders, looking every inch the radiant bride. "But I'd better get changed so we can meet the others for game night, and we still have a stalker to catch and a wedding to pull off."

Ellie laughed. "That's the determined spirit I love to see."

As Courtney slipped out of the gown and handed it to her sister, Ellie gazed at the beautiful wedding dress. She silently vowed that Courtney and Rufus would have the day they deserved.

Like their mother's love, Ellie's protective abilities flowed as an undercurrent through all she did. She would move heaven and earth to shelter her sister.

The dress seemed to glow in a beam of sunlight as Ellie carefully stored it away.

Touching Nana's string of pearls still around her neck, Courtney looked at her sister. "I just thought about the cabochon necklace."

Ellie looked up with an expression of shock on her face. "Why?"

"I remember how beautiful it was. Is it still in the safe?"

"Yes." Ellie busied herself putting away her sewing supplies. "And that's where it's going to stay."

"Do you ever take it out and look at it?"

"Absolutely not."

The necklace consisted of a simple silver chain with an oval cabochon containing a pearly white moonstone. It stayed in a white leather, lead box to keep its energy inside. That way no one could know where it was.

The necklace had belonged to the Roseland sisters' Nana, who then passed it on to the girls' mother. Elizabeth was wearing the necklace when she died after a hit-and-run accident in Boston.

Ellie said, "If the necklace is taken out of the box, then some people can sense where it is and come after it. Katrina gave her life protecting that necklace. It has to stay in the box, inside the safe. It can't see the light of day."

Katrina Stenmark, a keeper of the necklace, had once owned Jenna and Tom's house a couple of doors down from the Victorian. The older woman knew the cabochon had powers and that people were after it, so she gave it to the sisters' Nana for safekeeping. One night, someone broke into Katrina's house trying to find the necklace and when she wouldn't tell them where it was, she was killed.

"But you're its keeper now," Courtney continued. "Maybe if you take it out of the box, it could help keep all of us safe like it did when we were trapped in the carriage house fire years ago."

Ellie shut the door of her sewing cabinet. "I'm its keeper which means I have to protect it from evil hands, and I can only do that by leaving it inside its lead box in the safe. It can't come out … not ever."

It was clear the discussion about the necklace was over.

The sprawling Victorian mansion brimmed with warmth and laughter as the monthly game night began. Angie always looked forward to the fun evenings spent with friends and loved ones playing games, sharing stories, and enjoying delicious treats. It was a welcome respite from the craziness lurking outside.

That night, the crowd was larger than usual. Chief Martin and his wife Lucille chatted with Francine and her boyfriend on the plush living room sofas. At the dining table, Betty giggled at something amusing Mr. Finch whispered in her ear.

Meanwhile, in the kitchen, Angie and her bake shop manager Louisa put the finishing touches on the spread of appetizers and desserts to fuel the night's fun. Trays of coconut macaroons, chocolate espresso brownies, and pumpkin whoopie pies sat alongside a hearty veggie platter and bowls of mixed nuts.

"Everything looks delicious as always," Louisa said, heading to the counter for more wine glasses.

Soon the guests had filled their plates and settled in the living and dining rooms. Tom dealt cards for a rousing game of poker around the coffee table, and at a round table nearby, Ellie, Jack, and Lance— Louisa's husband—took out the Monopoly board.

"I call the race car," Lance announced, eliciting amused eye rolls from the others.

Meanwhile, Rufus and Josh set up Pictionary, while Lucille, Betty, and some of the B&B guests started an earnest game of Scrabble. The air was filled with playful competition and lively conversation.

Angie felt her stress melting away as she sank onto the sofa between Courtney and Jenna. "This was just what I needed tonight," she said contentedly, nibbling a brownie.

"Me, too." Courtney snuggled into Angie's side. "Although with the wedding getting closer, my mind keeps spinning."

Jenna gave her sister's knee a sympathetic pat. "Understandable. But Rufus will take good care of you." She nodded to where Rufus was fervently sketching something on the Pictionary pad, causing eager guesses from Josh and Chief Martin.

Courtney watched her fiancé with a smile. "He's been my rock. I honestly don't know how I'd get through this without him."

Angie hugged her sister close. "He sure is a good guy. He's already part of this family."

A sudden commotion arose from the Monopoly table. "Ha! Go directly to jail!" Ellie crowed, sending

Lance's race car token to the dreaded space as he groaned dramatically. "This hotel empire of mine is unstoppable."

"That's my ruthless businesswoman," Jack said, giving his wife a proud smile.

Tom shook his head. "I swear, Ellie's always had a knack for the game."

Jenna laughed. "Tell me about it. We knew better than to play against her as kids."

Just then, Chief Martin stood and clapped his hands for attention. "What do you all say to a game of charades?" Enthusiastic agreement greeted his suggestion.

Soon the group broke into teams, then Chief Martin consulted his watch. "The first team has three minutes ... go!"

Betty and Mr. Finch huddled, and then Betty stepped forward making decisive gestures. She pointed in turn to her eyes, then her hands, and then mimed flipping furiously through pages.

"Reading a book," Josh yelled out.

Betty shook her head, repeating the gestures more emphatically.

"Writing," Angie exclaimed. "Writing a book."

Betty nodded vigorously, holding up two fingers.

"Second word..." Courtney pursed her lips in

thought. Her face lit up. "Typing. You're typing a book."

"Yes! Nicely done." Betty gave Courtney an approving pat as she rejoined her teammates.

Next it was the wife of a B&B couple's turn. The husband and wife whispered back and forth heatedly about what to act out. Finally, the wife stepped up and positioned her arms as if holding a baby. Then she pretended to smell something gross and grimaced in displeasure.

Her teammates stared, stumped. "Changing a diaper?" Ellie guessed tentatively.

The woman shook her head no, repeating the awkward gestures. The other teammates frowned, equally confused.

"Oh, come on. It's so obvious," the wife exclaimed in frustration.

"Sorry, you've got us totally lost," Chief Martin said kindly.

The exasperated woman looked at her watch. "Ugh, time's up? It was rocking the baby."

Chuckles broke out as the teammates argued over the vague pantomime. Angie just smiled, enjoying the lively, competitive spirit of the game. It was nice to see everyone relaxing and having fun together.

The games continued late into the night, filled with theatrical performances, outrageous guesses, and lots of laughter.

When some of the guests reluctantly suggested it was time to leave and headed out into the night, Angie turned to Chief Martin as he finished helping Lucille with her light jacket.

"Any updates on the investigation?" she asked quietly, not wanting to dampen the cheerful mood. "Have there been any developments?"

The police chief hesitated before responding in a low voice. "As you know, Leeann Paulson and her fiancé decided to postpone their wedding indefinitely. After the last threatening gift, they were too afraid to hold the ceremony."

"We heard about that." Angie's stomach dropped. She exchanged an uneasy glance with Mr. Finch.

Chief Martin nodded grimly. "I'm concerned the stalker will be infuriated by the canceled wedding. He could lash out and..." His eyes flicked to Courtney and Rufus chatting across the room. "Take it out on Courtney and Rufus."

Angie's heart constricted as she swallowed hard. "What can we do?"

"I'm putting extra patrols on your street," Chief

Martin said, "and Officers Pike and Graham will be at the ceremony. Josh mentioned he's also hiring private security?"

"Yes, to watch the yacht the night before the wedding and monitor for any suspicious goings-on," Angie confirmed. She appreciated her protective husband's thorough precautions. "Security will also be at the ceremony and the reception."

Chief Martin nodded. "Try not to worry. We'll tighten the net and catch him soon."

While Josh and Chief Martin chatted quietly in the foyer, the others left, and Angie waved from the porch until the last taillights disappeared down the drive. Back inside, she found Courtney alone in the quiet kitchen tidying up. Angie wordlessly wrapped her in a fierce embrace.

Courtney returned the sudden hug, chuckling softly. "What's that for?"

Angie pulled back, her eyes serious. "For being the bravest, most loving sister imaginable."

18

The cheerful din from the festive game night still echoed through the Victorian's rooms as Chief Martin prepared to head home for the evening. He and Josh had lingered in the foyer, discussing final security precautions for Courtney and Rufus' upcoming wedding.

"I'll have undercover officers circulating during the reception, too," Chief Martin was saying. "The stalker won't get anywhere near—"

He was interrupted by the sound of the doorbell. The men exchanged a look of surprise.

"Who could that be at this hour?" Josh wondered aloud.

Chief Martin instinctively straightened as he

approached the front door. Peering through the side-light window, he visibly relaxed.

"It's Francine," he told Josh, opening the door to reveal the petite woman on the doorstep clutching a small box and an envelope.

"I'm so sorry to bother you," Francine said breathlessly, "but as I drove away, I noticed this package on the porch. It's addressed to Courtney."

She handed the box to Chief Martin, shooting an anxious glance back at her idling car by the street. "I thought you should have it right away, just in case." Her unspoken words hung ominously in the air.

"You did the right thing, Francine," Chief Martin said gravely, turning the package over in his hands. "Thank you. Please drive home safely."

With an uneasy smile, Francine hurried back to her car and soon her taillights disappeared down the street.

Chief Martin carried the box inside, holding it gingerly by the edges as if it might explode.

Angie, Courtney, and Rufus had been clearing away plates and cups left over from the party. At the sight of the chief's grim expression, the lighthearted mood evaporated.

"I heard Francine's voice. What did she want?" Angie asked.

Wordlessly, Chief Martin held up the small box. Shocked recognition flashed across Courtney's face.

"Francine found this on the porch. It's addressed to you," the chief said quietly.

Courtney sank into a chair, her face going pale. Rufus immediately moved to her side and took her hand. Angie stood frozen, dread coiling inside her.

Chief Martin carefully placed the box on the dining table. "If you don't want to open it, I understand..."

"Just tell me what it says," Courtney whispered, unable to tear her eyes from the package.

Nodding, Chief Martin pulled on a glove from his pocket before removing a small envelope affixed to the box. He opened it and read aloud, "A token of my esteem for you."

With a serious expression, he lifted the lid off the box. Nestled inside was a gleaming silver switchblade.

Angie gasped and her hand flew to her mouth. Rufus went rigid, his eyes blazing with rage. Euclid and Circe let out wild hisses.

"That monster," Josh burst out, smacking a hand on the table.

Footsteps pounded into the room as Ellie and Mr. Finch appeared with Jenna on their heels.

Taking in the scene, alarm flashed across their faces.

"What's happened?" Ellie demanded. Her eyes landed on the open box and she recoiled. "Oh no..."

Jenna hurried to Courtney's side, hugging her trembling shoulders. Mr. Finch and Ellie exchanged angry looks.

For several moments, no one spoke. The group simply stared at the knife nestled on top of some tissue paper, as if they were struggling to process the new threat.

Finally, Ellie broke the tense silence. "What does this mean? Is the knife for Courtney to protect herself, or..." She couldn't bring herself to finish the thought.

Mr. Finch slowly wiped his glasses with a handkerchief. "I'm afraid, Miss Ellie, this is meant as a threat."

Rufus spat out a harsh curse, his body riddled with fury.

Chief Martin carefully closed the box. "I'll need to take this back to the station to be processed for prints and trace evidence, but I promise you, we'll find this man and stop him." His jaw was set like granite.

Courtney finally tore her eyes from the table to look up at the chief. "I'm through cowering before this monster. No more reacting to his threats."

She stood abruptly, color returning to her cheeks as anger kindled behind her eyes. "I wish he would just come at me directly so we could end this." Her voice rang with conviction.

Striding closer to the box, Courtney declared, "Listen to me, you spineless coward. I'm not afraid of you. Show yourself and we'll give you the fight of your pathetic life."

A charged silence met her bold words. Then Rufus moved to Courtney's side, slipping an arm around her waist. "Here, here. That's the spirit." He glowered at the box as if it were the stalker himself.

Mr. Finch stepped forward as well. "Well said, my dear. We'll face the coward together."

Angie and Ellie exchanged nods.

"We'll be right by your side when he shows himself," Ellie vowed, her eyes flashing dangerously.

Josh said, "You got that right. He'll regret the day he targeted this household."

The shadow of a smile touched Courtney's lips as she took in her family's staunch support. She lifted her chin. "Bring it on. We're ready."

Chief Martin carefully gathered up the box and envelope as evidence, but privately, he worried the stalker's brazen act signaled an imminent confrontation. They had to locate the man before he could get to Courtney. "I'll expedite the processing on this," he told the group, "and we're going to surround the wedding with extra patrols." He held Courtney's gaze and gave her a nod.

After seeing the chief out, the family headed to the cozy kitchen. No one felt much like sleeping. Mr. Finch brewed chamomile tea while Angie sliced a coffee cake she'd baked earlier. A sense of comfort settled over them as they sat together at the long table.

Courtney allowed her stubborn facade to slip now that it was just family. She gripped Rufus' hand tightly, and he pressed a fierce kiss to her knuckles.

"No one's going to hurt you," Rufus declared. Around the table, the others echoed similar protective sentiments.

Courtney gave them a small grateful smile, but her eyes remained shadowed with worry.

Angie wished she could lift the fear and uncertainty that clung to her sister like a shroud, but all she could do was stay by Courtney's side and do her best to help protect her sister.

As if reading Angie's mind, Courtney met her gaze across the table. "Just having you all here with me makes everything seem less scary," she said softly. "Safety in numbers, I guess."

A lump formed in Angie's throat. On impulse, she rose and came around to hug Courtney tightly. One by one, the others joined the embrace until they stood encircled in each other's arms.

For several heartbeats, the kitchen fell silent, with the family members bathed in warmth and candlelight, drawing strength from one another.

Finally, they pulled apart, wiping at wet eyes and sharing smiles.

Mr. Finch sniffed and cleared his throat. "Well then. Who needs more tea?"

While some of them buzzed about preparing fresh cups, Angie watched her loved ones laugh and chatter.

And in several days time, Courtney and Rufus would stand together before their family and friends and declare their love ... flanked by their protectors.

At game night, Chief Martin had asked if a couple of the Roselands would visit Barri's two good friends,

Lisa Monty and Jen Bates, to talk to them about the stalker, and Angie and Courtney agreed to go.

"Rufus and I met Lisa at Leeann's pottery store the day we went to warn Leeann about the stalker," Courtney explained. "She's a potter like Leeann."

The next day, Lisa and Jen met the sisters at a cozy café in Silver Cove. Lisa had long auburn hair, brown eyes, and a stocky build while Jen had wavy black hair, brown eyes, and an average build. When Angie and Courtney arrived, they waved them over to their table by the windows, and introductions were made.

"Thanks for meeting with us," Courtney said as she and her sister took seats across from the young women. "We met at Leeann's pottery shop. Nice to see you again," she told Lisa.

"Yeah, you, too." Lisa nodded.

"We're sorry about your friend Barri. It seems she was a lovely person," Angie acknowledged.

"She sure was," Lisa said. "We can't believe she was killed. She was the kindest, sweetest person. I met her in grade school, and we were friends for over twenty years." Her voice turned hoarse with emotion, and she reached for her glass of water to take a long sip.

"I met Barri in middle school, and the three of us were like the Three Musketeers," Jen told them.

"We'd like to ask you questions about Barri and her life to get some insight into what happened to her," Courtney explained. "Had there been any trouble between Barri and someone? Any disagreements, arguments, a disgruntled customer, maybe?"

Jen and Lisa looked at each other.

"Except for her stalker, neither of us heard of any trouble. Barri would have told us if anything odd was going on. You know about the stalker, right?" Lisa questioned.

"We do," Courtney said with a nod. Not wanting the young women to know she was being targeted by the same person, she had to keep her emotions in check.

Jen said, "We really didn't take it as a threat. It was odd for sure, but none of us thought the person would turn violent. I'm so sorry about that. If we had taken it more seriously, Barri might still be alive."

"You didn't do anything wrong," Angie consoled them. "You had no reason to think the person would resort to violence."

"I think it was someone Barri knew," Lisa said. "She usually kept her doors locked. Someone she knew must have come to the door and she let him inside."

"If it was an acquaintance or a customer from her shop, do you think Barri would have let them in?" Courtney asked.

"She would have, yes." Jen nodded. "She wouldn't have been suspicious of someone she was familiar with. I don't think any of us would have been suspicious. We might wonder why the person came by, but I bet we would have opened the door to them."

"I think you're right," Angie agreed. "We know Barri was to marry Trevor Ralston. Can you tell us about her relationship with him?"

After looking at Jen, Lisa leaned forward. "Look, neither one of us liked Trevor. He wasn't a good match for Barri."

Jen said, "He was flamboyant and spent money like a drunken sailor. Initially, Barri thought Trevor had it all together. It took her a long time to figure out he was a phony. Barri was careful with her money. She was smart and sensible. Her parents taught her to save and invest. She wasn't really interested in material stuff. She and Trevor dated in high school. They broke up when they went to college but got back together when they came back to Silver

Cove after graduation. Trevor swept her off her feet. I think he really did love her, but I also think he was after her money."

"Did Barri have a lot of money?" Courtney asked.

Jen said, "She was a saver since we knew her as kids. If she got money as a birthday or Christmas gift, she put it in the bank. She started mowing lawns when she was only twelve and worked other part-time jobs as soon as she was old enough. She saved it all. When her grandmother died, she inherited twenty thousand dollars. It went straight into the bank. Barri had long-term plans for herself. She paid cash for the small building that houses her shop. She put down a lot of money on her house when she bought it." She looked over at her friend. "We should have followed Barri's lead when we were younger. We would be in better financial shape if we'd done what she did."

"Is it possible Barri was going to call off her wedding because of financial differences between her and Trevor?" Courtney questioned.

Jen and Lisa remained quiet for a few beats.

With a sigh, Jen said, "I guess it doesn't matter now if we share what she told us. Barri was sure she was making a mistake. She got cold feet about marrying Trevor. She was going to call him the night before the wedding and tell him she wanted to postpone."

Courtney and Angie looked at one another.

"It was going to be a very small wedding," Lisa piped in. "Only about thirty people. Trevor wanted a big extravaganza, but Barri insisted it would be a waste of money to do that. The ceremony and reception were going to be in her parent's barn, with flowers from their gardens and a simple buffet brunch. A friend was going to DJ the event. Barri was afraid to disappoint everyone if she canceled, but we told her to do what was right for her."

Courtney's heart was pounding. "Did Trevor go over to her house that evening?"

"We haven't talked to Trevor about it," Lisa told them.

"Do you suspect him?" Angie asked.

Jen's eyes widened. "You mean do we think he killed Barri?"

Angie nodded.

"Do *you* think he killed Barri?" Lisa asked.

"We're trying to help the police figure that out," Angie explained.

"We assumed it was the stalker who killed her," Lisa said, "but I admit to thinking it could have been someone else."

"Do you have any suspects in mind?"

"I'd just be guessing if I named someone," Lisa admitted. "I'd rather not."

"If you have any concrete suspicions, it could be very helpful to the case," Courtney advised.

Lisa took a quick glance at Jen, and then just shook her head and shrugged.

19

The moon was high in the night sky as Ellie drove her van along the winding coastal road toward the seaside town of Hamlet. Angie rode beside her in the passenger seat, while Courtney, Jenna, and Orla occupied the back. The cats were nestled on the floor at their feet. Orla had arranged a meeting with the powerful intuit Magill, who had helped the sisters when they were trying to solve their mother's murder.

Ellie's hands tightened on the steering wheel. "Why does Magill want me to bring the cabochon necklace tonight? Is she going to take it away from me? I'm supposed to be its keeper. I've done a good job keeping it safe. I don't want her to take it away from me."

Angie tried to reassure her sister. "Maybe she only wants to check on how you're doing keeping it from harm. I'm sure she just wants to check that you're protecting it properly." Though if she was being honest, Angie wasn't entirely certain of Magill's motives.

"What if she tries to take it from me?" Ellie said heatedly.

Jenna leaned forward between the seats. "No one is going to take it, Ellie. You're its rightful keeper now."

Ellie nodded, but her shoulders remained rigid. She took her duty to safeguard the powerful moonstone seriously.

Soon the car reached Magill Binney's rambling place that looked like a hobbit house. The wood-sided home had a thatched roof and a rounded glossy, wooden door. A lush green lawn sparkled in the moonlight, tall trees surrounded the house, and flower gardens were set on both sides of the home.

As Ellie parked, the front door opened, spilling warm light onto the porch. Magill's stocky figure appeared. She had gray, curly hair to her shoulders, big bright eyes, and a slightly stooped posture. She waved them inside.

The group soon settled around Magill's dining

room table with mugs of tea. Ellie kept the white leather box containing the necklace in her lap.

Magill turned her kindly gaze first to Courtney. "I know it's upsetting, but please tell me about the case of the stalker."

Courtney took a breath and reported on Barri's murder and the stalker's harassment of Leeann and herself. "Leeann feels unsafe so she and her fiancé have postponed their wedding. The stalker leaves us notes and small gifts. The last thing he left me was a knife."

Magill asked a few questions and then said, "I know troubling times have come upon you, but always remember, light still shines in the darkness for those with eyes to see it."

Courtney managed a small smile.

Jenna then relayed how she and Libby saw a ghost who gave them warnings. "I think the ghost is Barri come to warn Courtney. Libby saw the ghost in the backyard of the Victorian, and the spirit told her that Courtney and Rufus shouldn't be together... but that seems to be only part of the message. Libby told us the ghost was having a hard time communicating with her."

Magill listened intently.

"This spirit you saw must be Barri. I believe she

wishes to help, not harm. You'll hear from a spirit again," Magill said at last and then turned to Courtney. "You and Rufus are most definitely meant to be together. Heed the ghost's warning to stay safe, but do not fear. Your family will be your shield."

She looked to Ellie and asked her questions about her telekinesis and ability to sense things, and the young woman answered honestly.

"I understand you've begun to accept your skills." Magill searched Ellie's face.

"I want to be of service. I want to help."

Magill nodded. "I think you're ready to unlock stronger abilities that will aid you in protecting Courtney and Rufus. I think it's time for the cabochon to shine. It's time to take it from its hiding place."

A look of shock washed over Ellie's face as she shifted in her seat. She instinctively tightened her grip on the box. "You mean wear it?"

With a soft smile, Magill nodded.

"But if I wear it, it won't be protected by the lead box it's kept in."

"No, it won't," Magill replied gently. "It will be protected by you. The necklace's power has lain dormant too long. Its time has come again."

"I don't know if I'm ready for this," Ellie fretted.

"The ability to be humble is part of the reason you are its keeper," Magill pointed out. "You have come a long way over the past couple of years. You're accepting your skills, you've protected your family from harm numerous times, and your skills have developed. The time is right."

"But I don't know how to protect it." Ellie's lip quivered.

"Some things you have to discover for yourself," Magill told her. "You are ready." Sensing Ellie's uncertainty, Magill patted her hand. "Why don't we take this outside under the night sky? I've gathered some others who can reassure you."

Intrigued, the group followed Magill out to her backyard. Ellie's breath caught at the sight.

Tiki torches lined the yard illuminating a circle edged by tiny white lights woven through the trees. In the circle's center sat a small table holding candles and a dish of herbs and incense.

Shelby Price, a friend of Courtney's who had her own gifts, waited in the circle smiling, along with another woman they didn't recognize.

"Shelby!" Courtney hurried to her friend.

Shelby hugged Courtney and the other sisters, and introduced Fiona, a psychic and intuit who had helped her understand her own newly-discovered skills.

Magill said, "Shelby and Fiona are here tonight to represent your guardians and helpers, both seen and unseen. Their energy will surround you when you need it. Take heart and be brave."

Once inside the ring of torches, Shelby lit the candles, then lit the herbs and blew out the flames so wisps of smoke floated in the air around them.

Magill asked Courtney to open the white box. Inside, the cabochon sat on white satin and the moonstone looked opaque and dull.

A hush fell over the yard. The smoke and flickering flames lent an ethereal air to the gathering.

Magill told everyone where to stand and they formed a loose circle within the torches. Euclid and Circe were instructed to sit in the center of the circle next to the table.

Magill began to chant in a language none of them understood. She lifted the dish of herbs and moved it around so the smoke dispersed, then looked at each member of the circle.

"Each of you has special skills. You will use your skills to protect, assist, encourage, and support those around you. You will be grateful for your powers.

You are part of a whole that cannot exist without you."

Magill looked at Courtney. "Bring the necklace forward."

Courtney stepped into the center of the circle and stood before Magill cradling the open white box in her hands.

Magill lifted the necklace and faced Ellie who was standing next to her. The cabochon remained dull and clouded.

"This stone awaits your light," Magill pronounced. "You are the keeper. The powers of your mother, grandmother, and all who came before them now flow through you. Some have given their lives to protect this necklace. If called upon to save the cabochon, you will do the same. The moonstone commands great power. You will use it to do good. It will aid you in protecting your family from those who wish them harm."Magill held the cabochon up into the air. "Moonstone represents clarity and connection to the feminine. It is a symbol of light and hope and also encourages us to embrace new beginnings. It is closely linked to fertility, balance, softness, and intuition. Moonstone helps with physical, emotional, and spiritual healing. This necklace also contains a bit of mistletoe. Mistletoe holds its own magic. It's said to have healing properties and protects people from harm. It can protect against fire and is a symbol of love. There are many legends around the plant. The French used to think that if someone held a sprig of mistletoe, then they would be able to see ghosts and make them speak. The cabochon is its most powerful in the hands of a keeper, the protector of the stone."

Magill smiled at Ellie. "The stone knows who it should be with and right now, that's you. It glows and shimmers only when it is with its keeper."

Reverently, the woman placed the cabochon around Ellie's neck.

For a breathless moment, nothing happened. Then, before Ellie's amazed eyes, the moonstone began to glow from within, filling the yard with pearly light. The stone seemed to sparkle like a thousand stars, and the light was so bright it was almost blinding.

Gasps sounded around the circle. Ellie lifted the glimmering cabochon with trembling fingers, scarcely believing the transformation.

"Its power responds to you," Magill said, smiling. "You have unlocked its magic. Use it wisely in defense of those you love and for the people who need your help. You will learn to control the glow.

You will shield its power and energy so that others cannot find it. Wear it well, Ellie Roseland. Use it when necessary. You are now one with the stone."

Tears spilled from Ellie's eyes, and Euclid and Circe stared up at the moon and trilled their sweet song to the sky.

As they held one another's hands, the necklace glowed brighter.

Angie and Jenna wrapped their arms around their sisters, the four forming an impenetrable circle. Amidst murmured words of wonder, Ellie allowed her joyful tears to slip down her cheeks. She had found her purpose.

The smoke swirled as Magill began chanting again. Shelby and Fiona added their voices, weaving a melodic tapestry. The sound seemed to thrum through Ellie's veins.

When the chant ended, Magill came forward and pressed sprigs of mistletoe into each of their hands. "Remember, I stand with you. Call, and I will come."

Shelby and Fiona echoed this promise.

Just before they left the house, Magill whispered to Jenna, "You will see the ghosts again. They will help you protect Courtney and Rufus."

Then the woman took Angie's and Courtney's

hands in hers. "When the time comes, you will know what to do."

She smiled at Courtney. "I will be at your wedding to bless you and Rufus."

Back in the van, the women marveled over the empowering ritual.

As Ellie turned the ignition key, the necklace's glow faded to a faint shine so as not to draw unwanted attention, but she could still feel the thrum of its power.

"Mom and Nana would have been so proud," Jenna said softly from the backseat.

Overcome, Ellie could only nod, blinking back more tears.

The dark woods and coastline slid past the windows, but Ellie gazed straight ahead down their winding path home, her heart brimming with love. The light within her burned brightly now, holding the shadows at bay.

20

The cozy warmth of the Victorian's family room enveloped the sisters, Mr. Finch, and the cats like a hug as they gathered late that night to discuss the profound events at Magill's. A fire crackled merrily in the hearth and candles cast a soothing glow.

As Angie passed around mugs of tea and bowls of popcorn, Ellie kept glancing down at the moonstone pendant now resting against her chest. Though its brilliant illumination had dimmed, she could still feel it thrumming with dormant power.

"I'm so proud of you for being the cabochon's keeper," Jenna said, giving Ellie's hand an affectionate squeeze.

Ellie managed a timid smile. "It was incredible seeing it glow like it did when I first wore it. It isn't shimmering as strongly like it was. I'm already able to manage its brilliance. This whole thing is a bit terrifying. So much depends on me now. I don't want to fail and have it stolen by someone with evil intentions." She looked down at her hands as doubts crept back in.

Sensing her trepidation, Mr. Finch leaned forward with a look of kindness on his wrinkled face. "You needn't shoulder this alone, Miss Ellie. We are all here to support you." He ran his hand over the sweet black cat curled up on his lap.

"That's right." Angie wrapped an arm around Ellie. "Your struggles are our struggles, too."

The unconditional love and support of her sisters never failed to lift Ellie's spirits. She exhaled, feeling some of the tension leave her shoulders. "You always know just what to say. I don't know what I'd do without all of you."

"Well, you shall never have to find out," Mr. Finch pronounced staunchly. "We must remember that the moonstone is not a panacea and it can't do miracles, but it will amplify someone's paranormal skills and make them more powerful."

A companionable silence settled over the room for a moment as each became lost in their own thoughts. The crackling fire and the cats' steady purring soothed their frayed nerves.

Jenna broke the silence with a wistful sigh. "I can't stop thinking about the ritual. The candles, the torches, our joined hands ... it was so amazing." Her face took on a dreamy look.

Angie nodded slowly. "Magill's chanting and all of us standing together - I could feel everyone's energy empowering us. We're lucky to have so many allies."

"Allies who will have our backs if we need them," Ellie said. She vowed not to fail her family or the cabochon's legacy.

Mr. Finch gave her an approving pat on the knee. "Yes, indeed. And let's not forget, you have abilities of your own outside of the necklace's magic." His eyes twinkled behind his spectacles. "I daresay you could send that scoundrel stalker flying across the room with a mere thought."

Ellie flushed at the praise. It heartened her to know that, with or without the pendant, she had her own inner powers to draw on. She and her sisters had overcome terrible threats before and they would do so again.

Angie reminded her sisters, "The necklace isn't going to save us from everything. Mom was wearing it when she died, and it couldn't save her." Her voice trailed off, heavy with sadness.

A pang shot through Ellie's heart. Their mother's tragic death would always haunt them, despite the magic she'd worn around her neck. They could not rely wholly on the moonstone.

"You're right," Ellie said heavily. "The cabochon is an asset, but not a magic wand. We have to be smart." She touched the pendant. "I'll need to learn how best to use its power."

"Magill told me she'll be at the wedding to give a blessing to Rufus and me," Courtney explained. "She told me Rufus and I are meant to be together."

Euclid had been sitting next to the young woman, but he'd stood up and happily licked her face with his pink tongue.

Mr. Finch beamed. "I am so happy to hear this. If Magill is planning to attend the wedding ceremony, she must believe you and Rufus will not be harmed by the stalker."

"Speaking of the stalker," Angie said, "Courtney and I thought it was odd how Barri's friends didn't want to mention any suspects."

Jenna asked, "Could Jen and Lisa be afraid of repercussions if they mentioned someone's name in connection to Barri's death?"

"It's possible," Mr. Finch replied.

Courtney speculated, "Barri's sister Arlene seemed to harbor jealousy toward her sister, and her brother seems completely unattached to Barri emotionally. Maybe one of them argued with Barri over something, and the person lost their temper and killed her."

"And there's the fiancé Trevor," Angie noted. "He's in deep financial trouble. Barri's mom thought her daughter would be canceling the wedding. Barri and Trevor really weren't a good match."

"If Barri told Trevor she wanted to back out of marrying him, he could have become violent and in a fit of rage, killed her," Courtney said.

"But if one of Barri's family members killed her, why stalk Leeann and Courtney, too?" Jenna asked. "What could be the motivation?"

No one had an answer. They continued to be baffled.

"A few people seemed to have had motivation to kill Barri, but we're basing their actions on a burst of anger," Angie said. "Someone was stalking Barri with notes and gifts. That indicates premeditation, not a fit of rage."

"It's all too confusing." Jenna shook her head.

With a sigh, Courtney said, "Let's talk about

something happier." She walked over to the side table and picked up a folder, and then returned to the sofa. Her face glowed with excitement as she showed them printouts of the flower arrangements and table settings for the wedding.

"The florist just sent over the final plans." Courtney smiled softly.

Joyful tears pricked Ellie's eyes to see her sister's spirits lifted. She knew Courtney had worried the stalker's shadow might ruin their plans.

They passed the prints around admiring the lavish arrangements. "These will make the garden look like something from a fairy tale," Jenna breathed.

Courtney nodded. "Rufus and I want it to feel magical and full of love. A day for new beginnings." Her expression faltered slightly. "Do you ... do you really think we'll make it down the aisle safely?"

A lump formed in Ellie's throat. She reached out and took Courtney's hands in hers. "Look at me. I promise you, nothing will ruin your wedding day."

The others chimed in with their own vows that the ceremony would proceed undisturbed.

"Especially with Magill herself overseeing the blessed event," Mr. Finch pointed out brightly. "It is going to be a beautiful day."

Courtney's shoulders sagged in relief. "You're right. What was I thinking?" She laughed shakily. "I guess the stress has me worried about threats around every corner."

"Completely understandable, my dear." Mr. Finch smiled warmly. "By all the stars in heaven, we will keep you and your Englishman safe."

Courtney flashed him a grateful smile. The joyful wedding chatter continued.

As the others talked about the reception on the yacht, Ellie's hand drifted to rest on the hidden pendant around her neck. Its energy hummed against her skin.

Before heading home to her own house, Jenna stopped into her studio at the back of the Victorian to make a few notes for the next day. Euclid and Circe followed her into the room and jumped up on the sofa. Moonlight streamed in through the window, casting a pretty glow across the work table where glittering beads and stones had been spread out. The room felt cozy and peaceful.

Nearby on the sofa, the cats had settled contentedly, and Jenna smiled softly at the tranquil scene.

Setting down her pen, she tidied the pile of papers and her gaze fell on the sprig of mistletoe she'd received from Magill earlier in the evening.

Jenna lifted the sprig delicately by the stem, peering closely at the shriveled white berries. As she did, a feeling like warm honey flowed through her veins, relaxing her tense muscles and quieting her racing mind.

Placing the mistletoe back on the desk, Jenna exhaled slowly. Magill was right - the plant possessed its own subtle power. She made a mental note to keep it close in the days ahead.

A light began to shine in the corner of the room, and Jenna turned her head to see what it was. As she watched, stunned, Nana's ghost slowly took form with her translucent body shimmering and sparkling, and her kind eyes settling on her grand-daughter.

"Nana," Jenna breathed, scarcely trusting her eyes. How she'd longed to see her grandmother's comforting face over the past harrowing weeks.

Circe and Euclid let out delighted trills as they trotted over to sit at Nana's feet.

Joy leapt in Jenna's heart. She hadn't realized how much she needed this visit from the one person who had always offered help and comfort.

"Nana, it's so wonderful to see you." Jenna smiled through sudden tears. "We're worried about Courtney's and Rufus' safety. Someone is stalking Courtney. We don't have any concrete leads. We're having a hard time figuring out who it is. We don't know how to protect them."

Jenna searched her grandmother's translucent features, hoping for some sign from the spirit, but the ghost just looked at her, as if waiting.

Then Nana glanced over Jenna's shoulder at the shelf lining the wall behind her desk. Jenna followed her gaze, seeing nothing but jars of beads, jewelry tools, a few books, some sea glass, and several pearly shells.

When Jenna turned back around, her grandmother gave her a single, slow nod before gradually fading from view. The cats meowed at the spirit's departure.

Jenna released a shaky breath she hadn't realized she'd been holding. Though Nana hadn't spoken, her brief presence still filled Jenna with hope.

She studied the shelf her grandmother had indicated, searching for whatever sign or message might lay hidden there when she noticed a conch shell that had fallen sideways and went to stand it upright.

As she touched the spiral shell, a fragment of a

half-forgotten memory surfaced ... herself as a child listening to Nana explain how ancient peoples used shells to hear the ocean's wisdom.

Jenna's pulse quickened. On impulse, she held the conch to her ear. The hollow chamber magnified the sound of her own breathing as she listened for any murmur or whisper.

At first, all was quiet - then Jenna detected a faint sound, almost more of a sensation than a noise. Her skin prickled with goosebumps. Was some message stirring in the shell?

Jenna sank onto the sofa, her eyes slipping closed as she focused her full attention. There it was again - a barely audible buzzing, like voices just below the edge of hearing.

For the space of several heartbeats, she sat still waiting for a message of some kind, but then the fleeting murmurs faded. Jenna's eyes flew open, her own ragged breaths the only sound she could hear.

The conch shell slid from her fingers onto her lap. Though she hadn't understood the whispers, she knew that answers lay waiting for her. She only had to listen.

Looking around the empty studio, Jenna felt her grandmother's calming presence all around her. She stood and returned the conch to its place on the shelf. She would come back to it tomorrow, but for now, she held to the comfort her grandmother's visit had brought her.

With the cats trailing after the young woman, Jenna left the studio and headed for the backdoor off the kitchen. Before leaving the Victorian, she bent to stroke the cats.

"I'll be back tomorrow, sweet ones. We'll figure out everything soon."

21

Courtney, Angie, and Mr. Finch sat at the kitchen table and listened as Jenna reported seeing Nana in her studio the previous night.

"I was holding the sprig of mistletoe Magill gave us during the ceremony and as soon as I placed it back on my desk, glittering atoms shone in the corner of the room and Nana appeared." Jenna brushed at her eyes. "I was so happy to see her."

"Did she tell you anything?" Courtney was eager to hear what Nana might have told her sister.

"She glanced at the bookshelf by the windows and then she disappeared. I went over to the shelves and picked up the conch shell I keep there. I held it to my ear and I could hear murmurs, but I couldn't make out any words. I'll try again later today."

"Maybe Nana's hint didn't have anything to do with the conch shell," Courtney suggested. "Maybe there's something else on your shelves that can lead to a clue."

Jenna shook her head. "I'm pretty sure the conch shell is what I was supposed to pick up."

"I'm really glad Nana showed herself to you." Angie smiled. "I knew she'd try to help us."

"The message is unclear, but we'll figure it out." Jenna faced Angie. "What if we both sit with Mr. Finch later today and have another look at his sketches?"

Angie drew in a long breath, hesitant to experience another vision. "Okay. If it will help with this case, then I'm willing to try."

The late afternoon sun slanted through the windows of Mr. Finch's cozy apartment as Angie and Jenna settled in to examine his latest sketches. Euclid and Circe sat on the sofa in the sunroom across from the table and easels where the older man worked on his art. Today, the sisters hoped his artwork might shed light on the threats looming over Courtney's upcoming wedding.

"This book contains my most recent sketches." Mr. Finch laid a sketchbook on the table. "I used charcoal, my pencils, and some pastels. I tried to clear my mind and make quick sketches of whatever popped into my head."

Angie's face was a bit pale and her eyes looked worried.

"You'll be all right, Miss Angie," Mr. Finch told her. "We'll be sitting on either side of you. We won't let anything happen to you."

"I know." Angie gave a little nod. "I don't like having these visions, but I'm glad to help if I can."

"Shall we begin?" Mr. Finch asked as he took the seat next to Angie.

Jenna leaned forward and started to flip through the intricate sketches. Most depicted seascapes - rocky outcroppings lashed by foamy waves, weathered lighthouses, and fog-shrouded piers. Jenna paused at one rendering of a windswept beach scattered with seashells.

"These are remarkable as always," she said sincerely. "I can almost hear the crash of the surf."

"Thank you, Miss Jenna." Mr. Finch was about to go to the kitchen to prepare mugs of tea while the sisters continued examining the artwork, but he stopped when Angie spoke.

"Ooh, look at this one," Angie murmured. She held up a drawing of a conch shell half-buried in wet sand, its whorls gleaming. Something about the spiral shell tugged at her.

Jenna's eyes widened in recognition. "A conch shell, just like the one on my bookshelf."

Mr. Finch stood behind Angie's chair, peered at the sketch, and put his hand on her shoulder.

Angie's eyes never left the conch's intricately shaded spirals. She couldn't shake the sense that some vital message lay coiled in its chambers. If she just focused intently enough...

Suddenly, the sounds around her faded as Angie plunged deeper into the drawing. Mr. Finch and Jenna's indistinct voices seemed to echo from far away while she felt herself falling into the grey-toned artwork as her vision began.

Fog swirled, and then firm sand materialized underfoot as Angie found herself standing over a huge conch half-sunk on a windswept beach. The ridged shell felt solid beneath her fingertips when she reached out to touch it.

Angie knelt and lifted the conch to her ear. She could make out the same elusive sounds Jenna had described - muted murmurs lurking just below her understanding.

Like dust motes stirred by a sudden breeze, words began to filter from the shell's restless whispers. "Beware ... full moon ... keep them apart..."

Angie's pulse quickened. She strained to capture more word fragments, but the murmurs faded to a wordless sigh. Frustration welled up in her chest - she was so close.

Impulsively, Angie brought the conch to her lips and exhaled into its gleaming interior. The breath seemed to echo within the spiraling structure. When she listened again, the ghostly voices grew more distinct.

"...apart on the full moon's night ... when evil strikes ... keep them safe 'til dawn's first light..."

Suddenly a figure materialized out of the gloomy fog ahead of her - a silhouette of a figure whose rage warped their indistinct features. The figure was clutching a sinister blade.

Cold fear lanced through Angie. The stalker. In her vision, she took an involuntary step back, her pulse roaring in her ears.

When a hand grasped her shoulder, she heard Euclid and Circe meowing in the distance, and then the beach disappeared and she returned abruptly to the bright sunroom. Angie shifted unsteadily in her chair as Jenna and Mr.

Finch's concerned faces came into focus in front of her.

"Welcome back, my dear," Mr. Finch said, gripping Angie's shoulders to steady her as she found her bearings. "You went far away from us for a few moments there."

Angie leaned back against the chair as the strange vision continued to swirl through her mind. "I heard the cats. They were calling me back."

Circe and Euclid sat on the chair next to Angie, their eyes pinned on the young woman.

"They were howling and crying," Jenna told her.

Angie reached out to pat the felines as she haltingly recounted what she'd seen and heard in her vision to her sister and Mr. Finch.

Jenna's eyes widened. "So that's what Libby meant when she heard Barri's ghost tell her Courtney and Rufus couldn't be together. Part of the message got cut off. Courtney and Rufus can't be together on the night before the wedding. That's what Barri meant. But why can't they?" She trailed off with a shiver.

Mr. Finch's expression was grave. "We must keep Miss Courtney and her Rufus safely apart that night."

Angie nodded, her heart still fluttering against her ribs like a caged bird.

Mr. Finch gave her shoulder a gentle squeeze. "Steady now, Miss Angie. What you uncovered within the shell's whispers may well save lives."

As her adrenaline ebbed, Angie managed a weak smile, but her spine still prickled with unease. What might befall Courtney and Rufus under the full moon? They had only a couple of days to prevent whatever it was.

Jenna appeared rattled by the revelation. She stared at the conch shell in the sketch, her lips moving soundlessly as she pieced fragments together. Angie wished they could fully unravel the shell's warning and learn who was stalking their sister.

Abruptly, Jenna sat bolt upright, her gaze darting to the corner behind Angie. "Nana?" she uttered in an awed hush.

Angie whipped around but couldn't see anything.

There in the corner of the room, shimmering faintly, stood the spectral form of their late grandmother. The elderly woman offered Jenna an affectionate smile.

Hope surged in Jenna's heart. Nana had returned

to help guide them, but her joy dimmed when she noticed a second ghost hovering silently at Nana's side - a striking young woman with pale blonde hair.

"Barri," Jenna breathed. This was the restless spirit who had come to warn of impending danger. She shivered, irrationally uneasy in the presence of the two ghosts.

Nana floated closer and with a gentle look that contrasted with the seriousness of her message, she whispered to Jenna's mind, "Keep them apart. On the full moon's eve, keep them apart."

Suddenly, the apartment's window shades all crashed down, plunging them into shadow. Nana and Barri slowly faded away.

Jenna blindly groped for Angie and Mr. Finch's hands, her pulse thundering in her ears.

Mr. Finch hurried to put up the shades. As the apartment brightened, he turned to the shaken sisters, his own face pale.

Jenna told them that Nana and Barri had materialized and warned her that Courtney and Rufus must be kept apart the night before the wedding.

"You both heard the spirits' warnings. We know what we must do." Mr. Finch held Jenna and Angie's trembling hands in his weathered grip.

22

With Angie, Courtney, and Mr. Finch in the passenger seats, Ellie drove her van a few miles north to her and Jack's new development. Each step of the project had been full of setbacks and delays, but finally, ground had been broken for the first three townhouses they were investing in. It was hard for first-time buyers and people wanting to downsize to find a suitable home in town due to high prices. Ellie and Jack had been determined to find a way to make homes more affordable for people who wanted to remain in town after decades of living in Sweet Cove and for those who hoped to enter the market.

Ellie pulled the van into the tiny gravel lot and the three sisters got out. It was a warm late afternoon with a bright blue sky and a few wispy clouds passing by overhead.

"Wow." Courtney looked out to where the cellar holes had been dug for the townhomes. "It's really happening."

"It sure is." Ellie's face beamed. "Come on. Let's walk around."

Angie liked the layout of the new development. There would eventually be winding paths through the neighborhood for walking or cycling, and one path to the side led to the state park trails into the woods. Lots of trees remained and there was a central green space for kids to play or adults to meet up with friends.

Ellie carried her tablet with her so she could show her sisters and Mr. Finch the different phases of the project. "We're so excited that phase one is underway. Now that the cellar holes have been completed, the actual townhouses can start to go up."

"It's going to be wonderful," Mr. Finch said as he walked next to the tall young woman.

"We've already had lots of inquiries from people who are interested in moving here," Ellie continued. "Jack and I are thinking we might have to do a lottery to fairly choose who gets the places. We're still looking into the legalities of doing the sales that way."

Courtney smiled at Ellie. "You're really creating something of value here, and I don't mean that in a monetary sense. I mean you're going to provide affordable homes with great layouts and a beautiful setting to people who are struggling to buy something in their price range."

"That's exactly what Jack and I hoped to be able to do." Ellie walked them around part of the future neighborhood pointing out where other homes would go. "We'd really love to build a community building so people can hold bigger parties, gatherings, and classes and events of different kinds, but that's a future thing. We have to see how things go."

"It's been a great deal of work," Mr. Finch stated, "but the fruits of your labor are now blossoming. It's wonderful to see. We're very proud of you."

Ellie gave the older man a hug. "Are we going to practice here tonight?"

Ellie, her sisters, and the men had been practicing in the development some nights with Mr. Finch, who was trying to teach them to keep their heads in a fight, evade an attacker, plan what to do next when there were only moments to act, and how best to engage with someone bent on hurting you.

"Why don't we take the night off," Mr. Finch suggested. "I think we might take an hour tonight to discuss how we will communicate with one another when trouble shows itself, what to do if a plan isn't going well, how to come to someone's rescue, and things like that. If someone attacks, each of us has skills we can use to fight back or outwit the perpetrator, but there are many little things that could go wrong that we need to think about."

They all agreed those were very important pieces to consider.

As they walked back to the van, Mr. Finch asked Ellie if they might have time to stop on Main Street before returning home so he and Courtney could check on the employees at the art gallery and candy shop to see if anything was needed.

Ellie told them, "I don't mind stopping. I'm not in any hurry to get back."

Moving down Main Street, they were lucky someone was vacating a parking spot on the street just as they approached. Ellie skillfully maneuvered into the spot and cut the engine.

Ellie and Angie walked around inside the art gallery admiring the paintings on display while Courtney and Mr. Finch talked with the two employees about their shifts. Someone was coming in a little later to put on an introduction to painting workshop and they wanted to check that everything was all set.

When they were satisfied the event would go well, they all headed to the candy shop. One employee had called out sick for the evening shift so Courtney made some calls to other staff members to find someone who could fill in.

Mr. Finch made sure there was enough cash in the drawer and that the shelves and glass display cases were well-filled and ready for the evening rush.

"Are these new?" Angie looked inside one of the cases at the cake pops on display.

"They are, indeed," Mr. Finch replied. "We have some interesting flavors. Would you like to try one?"

"I'd like the red one, please," Ellie told him while Angie chose the lemon covered in white chocolate.

"That's red velvet with a raspberry and chocolate icing," Mr. Finch said handing the pops to the sisters.

"Delicious." Ellie took another bite.

"Mine is, too," Angie said. "I love this flavor combination. It's yummy."

When Courtney had finished her tasks, the four of them headed out to the sidewalk, where they decided to stroll past the shops for a little while before returning home.

They stopped and looked in the display window that had handmade headbands, jewelry, and other hair accessories.

"That headband is so pretty. See the one with the pearls and crystals? It would look great with our bridesmaid gowns," Ellie pointed out.

"Maybe we should take a look." Courtney led the way inside and the three young women spent a few minutes checking out the headbands. "I don't know. They're pretty, but Jenna told me she could put together barrettes with pearls, crystals, and a bit of ribbon for us. She said she could whip them up in about two hours. I think I'd like her to make them for us."

Ellie and Angie agreed and they returned to the sidewalk to continue their stroll.

A few shops down, a hurried young woman with long auburn hair emerged from a store and almost plowed into the Roselands and Mr. Finch.

"Oh, Lisa, hi," Angie said when she recognized Barri's friend from their meeting with her and another close friend to discuss the case.

"This is Lisa Monty. She was a good friend of Barri Lewiston." Angie introduced Lisa to Mr. Finch, who shook hands with her and offered his condolences. "And this is our sister, Ellie."

Ellie smiled and shook hands with the young woman.

"How are you?" Courtney asked her.

"I'm okay." Lisa's manner was a tiny bit brusque, like she was sorry to have run into the sisters. "I've been looking at small spaces to rent so I can open a store."

"What sort of shop are you going to open?" Mr. Finch asked.

"I haven't decided yet, but I want to do something. I feel like I'm stuck in place. I need to move forward with my life. I need something new." Lisa sighed. "Barri's death showed me we have to grab life by the horns. We can't be putting things off."

Angie said, "Lisa works at Leeann Paulson's pottery shop in Silver Cove."

"Not anymore. I quit that job. I want to work for myself."

"Well, good luck with whatever you decide," Ellie told her.

Courtney asked, "Have you given any more thought about suspects in the case? It seemed when we talked last you might have had some ideas. Maybe we could meet again and talk about it?"

Lisa shook her head. "I haven't thought of anyone. It wouldn't be helpful to meet. I need to get going. I have an appointment." The young woman waved as she turned away and hurried down the street.

"She sure seems like she doesn't want to talk to you about Barri's murder," Ellie pointed out.

"We wondered if someone might have threatened her to keep her quiet," Courtney explained.

"We also wondered if she was protecting someone," Angie said.

"She certainly seems like an unhappy person," Mr. Finch noted. "When I shook her hand, I picked up a lot of negative emotions from her. You might be right that she's keeping something from you because she's frightened or trying to keep someone from being named a suspect. Perhaps, you can contact her one day to set up another meeting. If you wait a week or so, she might be ready to talk."

Courtney looked down the sidewalk in the direction Lisa went. "That's a good idea. I sure wish she'd tell us what she knows."

23

A taxi cab rolled to a stop before the sprawling Victorian mansion, having brought passengers Rufus, Earl, and Susan Fudge from the train station. Susan and Earl flew into Boston from England and took the train to Sweet Cove, where Rufus met them at the station.

The English couple stepped out and surveyed the beautiful home where their son would soon be wed.

"What a magnificent old place," Earl remarked in his melodic British accent, admiring the stately architecture. At his side, Susan clasped her hands in delight, her wooden bracelets gently clacking together.

Before the cab could even pull away, the front

door burst open and out poured the four Roseland sisters and the two cats. Laughing with joy, the young women surrounded the visitors with warm hugs.

"Mum, Dad, welcome to the Victorian," Rufus exclaimed.

As he turned to make introductions, everyone shook hands and shared words of welcome. In his mid-sixties, Earl's refined manners lived up to Rufus' accounts of his father's London upbringing.

Also in her sixties, Susan's smile radiated warmth. Though born and raised in Connecticut, years living abroad had lightly touched her speech. Her festive floral skirt, slim figure, and pleasant smile projected a sweet, outgoing, and positive personality.

Susan had gone to school at Oxford, where she met Earl and received a degree in law. She'd worked for decades as a solicitor at a law firm. Earl had studied Greek and Roman civilizations and worked as a professor. Several years ago, they both retired and now spent time traveling around the world.

"It's wonderful to finally meet you both," Courtney said sincerely. Earl smiled brightly and shook her hand in his slender grip while Susan pulled her into an impulsive hug.

"The pleasure is ours," Susan declared. "Rufus has told us so much about you. Welcome to our family, dear girl."

Courtney flushed, blinking back joyful tears.

Spying the sisters hanging back, Susan rushed over to fold them into an embrace.

As Earl happily shook hands all around, the cats wound between their ankles, assessing the newcomers. Susan laughed with delight when Euclid deigned her worthy of an ear scratch.

Chatting merrily, the group moved inside to the living room for tea and cake. While Earl and Susan relaxed from their travel, the sisters peppered them with questions about their lives in England. Though reserved, Earl's pride over his son's wedding shone through.

Before Ellie showed the couple to their rooms to freshen up before the rehearsal, Susan squeezed her future daughter-in-law's hand. "I hope you know what a rare gem our son has found in you," she said softly.

Courtney ducked her head, her cheeks pink. She felt surrounded by love and family. For the first time, the shadows threatening their joy felt like they could be beaten. Tomorrow would be a celebration of their bright future to come.

The late afternoon sun warmed the Victorian's lush backyard as the group assembled for the wedding rehearsal. The garden was transformed for the special occasion with garlands of flowers decorating a white wooden arbor that would serve as the altar, and rows of white chairs separated by the aisle. A billowing white tent stood over the chairs to protect the guests in case of rain or hot sun.

Chief Martin, who would officiate the ceremony, took his place under the arbor, and then the procession began. First, Rufus escorted his mother Susan down the aisle to her seat in the front row. He returned to the back as the groomsmen - Jack, Tom, and Josh - started their walk, with Rufus following behind them.

Next came Libby and Gigi as flower girls, pretending to carefully drop flower petals, and then Ellie, Jenna, and Angie as the matrons of honor.

Finally, Mr. Finch proudly walked Courtney down the brick path. She grinned excitedly at Rufus waiting for her under the arbor's flowers. Though not official, walking the aisle created a sense of joy and anticipation for the real ceremony tomorrow.

After a quick run-through of the vows, the group

admired the beautifully decorated garden. Courtney clung to Rufus' arm, feeling happy to have rehearsed their ceremony as bride and groom and enjoying the pre-wedding cheer.

After the successful rehearsal, the family left the Victorian and walked up Beach Street to Main Street headed to the Pirate's Den restaurant owned by their friends for a delicious celebratory dinner. As they walked along the brick sidewalks, Susan admired the shops, pubs, and cafes they passed by.

The quaint seaside town of Sweet Cove sparkled under the afternoon sunlight as the Roseland family, along with Susan and Earl, gathered for an early dinner. After a lively wedding rehearsal in the backyard, they were all hungry and eager to relax over some tasty food in the company of friends and family.

The sprawling two-story Pirate's Den overlooked Sweet Cove's Main Street, offering nice views of the town. A jaunty animated pirate greeted them at the polished doors. Inside, nautical paraphernalia crammed the walls alongside photos of local sailing teams. Their large party was shown upstairs to an oval table perfect for mingling.

Courtney and Rufus sat at the head of the table in the private room, still excited from their practice walk down the aisle. In less than twenty-four hours, it would be official.

Angie ensured Courtney and Rufus were seated next to his visiting English parents, and the happy couple beamed with joy.

"We're tickled to be here celebrating our son's special day," Earl announced jovially in his melodic accent, giving Rufus an affectionate tap on the back.

Susan grasped Courtney's hand. "We're so happy to have a daughter now. We always hoped our Rufus would find someone special."

Earl and Susan's joy at their son's marriage was plain to see, and they soon had the table laughing at witty stories from Rufus' childhood.

Angie enjoyed watching her sister soak up the lighthearted pre-wedding moments. She knew the weight on Courtney's mind - they all carried it, but tonight, they pushed the worry away.

Once the food arrived, conversation faded into satisfied murmurs and the clink of cutlery. Angie's mouth watered at the savory bouillabaisse, a specialty of the coastal town. Mr. Finch relished his vegetarian risotto while Betty loved her haddock in white sauce.

Across the table, little Libby and Gigi whispered

and giggled together, clearly thrilled to be included. Angie beamed, her heart full to bursting.

After delighting in the restaurant's famed cannolis for dessert, the group reluctantly left the cozy Pirates' Den. The sun was heading to the horizon and the air was warm and pleasant as they ambled down Main Street, passing by Courtney and Mr. Finch's candy store.

"Do you remember the day we met?" Courtney asked. "We were right here outside the shop."

Rufus smiled down at her. "The second I saw you, I could hardly breathe, and when you looked at me, it felt like everything around us was sparkling."

Their sweet moment was interrupted by Angie saying, "Let's go down to Coveside and show your parents the harbor walk." Clasping Earl and Susan each by an elbow, she enthusiastically steered them toward the picturesque waterfront district.

There, gas lamps lit the winding cobblestone walkways lined with tidy shops and cozy cafes. Garlands of twinkling lights were strung overhead, setting a festive mood. The salt-tinged air carried notes of freshly caught seafood and steaming chowder.

Earl and Susan exclaimed over the charming storefronts as the group ambled leisurely along.

They sampled fudge at Edith's old-fashioned candy counter and looked at nautical antiques at The Crow's Nest.

With twilight deepening, Rufus and Courtney led the way back to town, passed the Victorian, and strolled to the beach at the end of the lane where they stood gazing out at the sea and watching the waves roll in and out.

"This is just beautiful." Susan sighed and slipped her hand through her husband's arm, her silver-streaked hair brushing his cheek as she leaned into him contentedly.

Angie's heart warmed at their romantic silhouette against the dark blue water. On her other side, Courtney mirrored the cozy pose with Rufus, her head nestled in the crook of his shoulder. Rufus pressed a kiss to her hair. "We'll bring our children here one day to splash and play in the waves."

Angie allowed them a moment of privacy before gently reminding them of the time. "It's getting dark."

"We need to go inside," Ellie told them.

As the group slowly wandered back up the street, a bittersweet weight pulled at their hearts. Soon, the two lovebirds would have to separate for the night.

Back at the Victorian, Josh and Jack prepared tea

and served cupcakes of various flavors in the living room, where Earl entertained them with a rousing piano recital and Susan passed around photos of young Rufus from their travels.

The warmth in the room made Angie feel bad about disrupting it, but they couldn't ignore the psychic warnings. As laughter rang out at a picture of gap-toothed Rufus in some sort of costume, she met Jenna and Ellie's eyes across the room, seeing her own reluctance reflected back from them.

Angie rose and cleared her throat. "Rufus, I hate to say it, but..."

Rufus' smile faded as understanding dawned across his face. He nodded, his jaw tightening. "It's time to say goodnight."

Earl paused his lively piano melody and Susan lowered her photos onto her lap, her brows knitting together.

"Is something wrong?" Susan asked in concern.

Courtney opened her mouth, but no words came out. How could she explain the supernatural warnings for Rufus and her to stay apart?

Sensing her distress, Mr. Finch intervened smoothly. "Forgive us, we should have mentioned - it is rather poor luck for the bride and groom to see one another on the night before their wedding."

This elicited nods of comprehension from Earl and Susan.

"Of course," Earl remarked.

Courtney flashed Mr. Finch a grateful look and turned to Rufus, her eyes swimming. "One more night apart."

"And then we'll be husband and wife." Rufus drew her close for a minute, and when he pulled back, his own eyes glistened.

With an affectionate meow, Euclid wound himself around Rufus' ankles, as though reminding him they must be going. Circe echoed the sentiment as she rubbed against Courtney's legs.

As the family ringed Courtney and Rufus in embraces, Angie hoped they had interpreted the unusual warnings accurately. She clung to hope that keeping the couple separated tonight would thwart the threat.

As Jack, Ellie, and Euclid ushered Rufus to the carriage house apartment as planned, Circe followed Courtney up to her suite of rooms.

Watching them go, Angie tried to swallow her fear ... and silently prayed that everyone would still be here tomorrow, safe and sound.

24

No one could sleep, and one by one, everyone except Courtney and Rufus' parents came down to the kitchen. Tension crackled in the air as Angie stood at the window looking out into the rear yard. Chief Martin had stationed an officer at the front of the house and one in the backyard. Still, Angie was on edge.

Jack, Ellie, and Euclid would be staying the night with Rufus in one of the carriage house apartments, and Gigi and Libby had gone to Orla and Mel Abel's house for a sleepover to keep them out of harm's way.

"I hope everyone in the carriage house is getting more sleep than we are." Jenna carried a mug of tea over to her twin and joined her in looking out the window. "Why does it *not* make me feel better that there are two police officers in our yard?"

Angie smiled. She'd been thinking the very same thing.

Mr. Finch sat at the table playing solitaire while Tom read a crime thriller novel and Josh worked at a crossword puzzle. Circe sat on the cat tree near the other kitchen window staring outside. Every few minutes, she would jump down and patrol around the house before returning to her station in the kitchen.

"Why do Courtney and Rufus need to stay apart anyway?" Jenna asked.

Mr. Finch looked up from his cards. "I believe the reason is if they're separated from one another and one is attacked, the other one will be able to come to help. If they're both in the same room, the attacker could hurt both of them at once."

"I guess that makes sense," Jenna admitted.

Mr. Finch said, "There isn't any use in all of us being awake. Why don't we split into shifts? Half of us can nap, and the others will stand guard. Then we'll swap positions."

"That's a good idea," Angie admitted. "I probably won't sleep, but at least I can lie down and try to rest."

"Why don't you go up to your room, Miss Angie?" Mr. Finch suggested. "I'll stay up for the first part of the night."

"I'm going up to Courtney's room to stay with her," Jenna said and turned to Tom. "Why don't you try to get some rest?"

Tom stood and yawned. "Okay. Ellie told me the small guest room at the top of the staircase is empty. I'll go in there and lie down for a little while, but I know I won't sleep."

All the guest rooms were empty that night because Ellie wanted the house to themselves before the wedding.

Josh said, "I'll stay with Mr. Finch."

Tom, Jenna, and Angie climbed the stairs and headed to the bedrooms, and despite feeling exhausted and anxious, Angie fell asleep the minute her head hit the pillow ... and she began to dream.

It was midnight, the moon was full, and Angie stood in the front yard, her eyes darting all around. Fog started to roll in off the ocean, and as she walked through the mist, she saw one of the officers turn around and smile, a smile that looked like a snarl.

Angie blinked and he was gone. She continued to walk slowly around the mansion and to the rear yard. She could see Rufus at the second-floor window of the carriage house looking down into the yard, flicking sparks from the end of his fingers, and she breathed a sigh of relief that no one had tried to attack him.

A wave of despair suddenly washed over Angie and her heart began to race.

She wheeled about trying to find the source of her anxiety. Two police officers lay in the grass unconscious. Angie stared through the fog at the Victorian and took off at a run, but she tripped and fell. When she tried to right herself, someone pushed her down from behind, kicked her, and pointed a knife at her throat.

Angie bolted upright in her bed, panting. She threw back the covers, ran from the room, thundered down the stairs, and rushed into the kitchen.

Josh and Mr. Finch looked up with wide eyes.

"What's wrong?" Josh hurried to his wife's side.

Angie's face was pale and her voice sounded hoarse. "It's starting. Someone is in the house."

Josh inhaled sharply. "Do you know where he is?"

"No." Angie looked close to tears.

Mr. Finch stood. "We all know what to do. Keep to our training. Focus. Open the group chat on our phones. Tom is guarding the second floor. I will stay here in the kitchen. Josh will monitor the rear of the house from the hallway that leads to the family room, my apartment, Miss Ellie's office, the door to the basement, and Miss Jenna's studio. Miss Angie will take the front of the house keeping watch over the living and dining rooms and the sunroom. I will alert Rufus, Miss Ellie, and Jack via text message. Take your places, keep your wits about you."

Everyone moved swiftly through the house to their positions.

Josh hurried to the hallway where he stood next to the door to the basement. In a moment, he thought he heard sounds coming from down there. He jumped when Circe rubbed against his leg.

He knelt on the floor and patted the cat. "Do you hear it, too?" he whispered to the feline.

Circe made eye contact with him and pawed the door.

"I'm taking that as a yes." Josh took out his phone and texted the others. Two minutes passed and Angie arrived at his side.

"Jenna and Courtney are locked in her room. Tom is standing guard at the top of the staircase."

A text came in on both of their phones.

"It's Ellie," Angie told Josh. "Rufus has left the carriage house and is heading for the basement."

"Oh, no. He should stay in the carriage house," Josh replied. "Is the bulkhead door to the basement locked?"

"Rufus will just set the wood around the lock on fire and get in that way."

"Let's go down to the basement." Josh quietly opened the door.

Suddenly, they heard the squeak of the bulkhead door that led outside from the basement as it opened. Then they heard a metallic crash, a shout, and a scream.

Angie held her pepper spray in one hand as they descended the stairs. Josh grabbed a wrench from the workbench and using the flashlight on his phone, they hurried through the dark cellar to the door to the rear yard. When they turned the corner, they saw a figure on the cold cement floor.

Circe darted ahead.

Angie cried out, "Rufus!"

Blood pooled on the floor from a gash on the back of the unconscious young man's head. Josh removed his shirt, balled it up, and used it to press against the wound.

Angie called for an ambulance and texted the rest of the family. "Is he breathing?" her words caught in her throat as tears tumbled down her cheeks.

"I feel a faint pulse. He's losing a lot of blood."

Circe looked up and hissed, then she took off for the staircase that led to the first floor of the Victorian.

"Oh, no, Josh! Whoever did this must have gone up to get at Courtney!" Angie stood. "Stay with Rufus." She ran for the stairs.

Josh heard a noise behind him and jumped to his feet, but sighed with relief when he saw Ellie and Euclid coming toward him from the bulkhead door.

"Is he alive?" Ellie kneeled next to Rufus while Euclid darted off upstairs.

"Josh! Where are you?" Mr. Finch called from the other side of the basement.

"We're here." Josh alerted the man.

Ellie looked up as Mr. Finch came around the corner. "I just got here. Rufus' pulse is faint. What should I do?"

Mr. Finch reached down to touch the unconscious young man. "You can help him, Miss Ellie. You can lessen the extent of his injury."

"I don't know how," Ellie wailed.

Mr. Finch took her hands in his. "Yes, you do, and you have the necklace to help. You are Elizabeth's daughter. What once beat in her heart, now beats in yours."

Ellie's voice trembled. "What do I do?"

"Put your hands on Rufus. Close your eyes." Mr. Finch spoke gently. "Focus on your energy. Let it flow through you. Concentrate on sending your energy through Rufus. You can do it, Miss Ellie. You've always had the power to do it."

Ellie gave a slight nod and placed both palms against Rufus' chest. She tried to slow her breathing, and little by little, she could feel her energy growing stronger. She thought about the cabochon she wore around her neck; it was glowing and pulsing against her skin. She concentrated on sending healing energy into Rufus' body. Her hands began to feel hot as they pressed against the young man.

"The bleeding has stopped," Mr. Finch said with a joyful voice.

"His pulse is stronger," Josh told them.

Rufus' eyes blinked open. "What's ... what's going on?" he managed to ask.

Tears streamed down Ellie's face, and Mr. Finch

wrapped his arms around her. "You did it, Miss Ellie, you did it."

Angie raced through the hall, into the foyer, and up the beautiful wood staircase to the upper floors.

At the landing, she saw Tom lying on his side, unmoving. She bent to feel for a pulse. He was alive but was bleeding a little from a wound on the side of his head.

She heard Jenna scream, and with her heart pounding like a jackhammer, she ran to Courtney's suite of rooms. The door was open, Jenna was on her knees clutching her arm, and someone wearing a black ski mask had Courtney in a bear hold with a knife to her neck.

Angie glanced at her twin who shook her head to indicate she didn't need help with her injury.

Angie took a step forward. "Drop the knife."

"Shut the door. Lock it." The person ordered Angie.

It was a woman's voice. Angie went to the door and pretended to turn the bolt, then turned around and noticed strands of long auburn hair sticking out from under the mask.

"Lisa," she whispered. "The police are on their way. Don't do this. Don't add to your troubles."

Courtney's hands were near her neck trying to protect her throat, but Lisa had a strong hold on the young woman.

"Why are you doing this?" Courtney asked in a small voice.

"Because you, Barri, and Leeann always get everything you want. I never do. I killed Barri. I admit it." Lisa's voice was hard, frantic, and rambling. "I wanted to own a shop. I wanted to be a well-respected potter like Leeann. I dated Trevor before Barri did. I loved him. She stole him from me. She had everything and I had nothing. Barri was so greedy. She deserved to die."

"Courtney never did anything to you," Jenna said through gritted teeth. "Let her go."

"She's just like Barri ... successful, pretty, in love with someone who loved her in return, about to get married." Lisa yanked the ski mask off her face and a sickening smile spread over her mouth. "But now, your lover boy is dead. I killed him. You'll never be together. You'll be miserable and alone like I always am."

As fury spread over Courtney's face, her lips trembled.

"She's lying," Angie told her sister. "Rufus is alive."

Lisa's eyes narrowed. "You're the one who's lying. I hit him."

Angie shook her head. "He's alive, Courtney. Rufus is alive."

Jenna noticed swirling atoms in the corner of the room and slowly, they formed into a shimmering woman. Nana. The ghost looked at Jenna and held up her fingers: 1, 2, 3.

Jenna understood. She looked to Angie from her position on the floor and mouthed the numbers 1, 2, 3. Angie nodded and as she took a step to the side to distract Lisa, Jenna looked at Courtney and held up her fingers: 1, 2, 3.

Courtney gave her sister the slightest of nods.

"One," Angie said in a loud voice.

"Two," Jenna's voice was nearly a shout.

"Three!" Mr. Finch said from behind the closed door before flinging it open.

At the same time, Ellie, wearing the cabochon necklace stepped into the room, Circe flew from her hiding spot behind a chair and flung herself onto Lisa's back, and Euclid raced toward Lisa to help.

Courtney used her elbow to smash Lisa in the

ribs and then fell to the floor and rolled out of the woman's grasp.

Ellie reached out her arms, her long hair rising up all around her head, floating in the air. Focusing on the knife in Lisa's hand, she used her telekinesis to twist it into a ball.

Lisa looked at the knife in her hand like it was a poisoned serpent and flung it to the floor, then pulled a second knife from her back pocket and ran at Courtney like a mad woman.

Ellie raised her hands again, but she didn't need her magic this time. Rufus' mother Susan was in the room now with her hand outstretched, and a bolt of fire flew from her fingertips and smashed Lisa in the chest. The young woman screamed and fell to the ground.

Ellie wheeled around and stared open-mouthed at Rufus' mother.

"Yeah," Susan said. "I have fire power."

25

Lisa was read her rights and taken into custody by Chief Martin. An ambulance transported Rufus to the hospital with Courtney and his mother riding with him. The young man's initial injury had been lessened and healed by Ellie, and he was checked by the doctors and released. Tom had suffered a good bonk on the head, and like Rufus, had a horrible headache, but was cleared by the medical team and sent home.

Lisa had used a knife to cut around the lock on the bulkhead door, but before that, she pretended to be someone from an area all-night restaurant who was asked to bring coffees and some donuts to the two officers watching the outside of the Victorian.

The drinks were drugged, and within fifteen minutes, the officers were out cold. That's when Lisa entered the mansion through the bulkhead.

When Rufus saw the opened door to the basement, he knew someone had broken in that way and raced inside to the cellar. Lisa was hiding. She charged the young man from behind and whacked him hard in the head.

When Angie and Josh went down to the basement, Lisa quietly snuck up to the first floor and took the stairs to the second floor. When Jenna heard the tussle in the hall between Lisa and Tom, she opened the door to Courtney's room to help her husband. By then he was unconscious, and Lisa attacked Jenna, resulting in the young woman breaking her arm.

Lisa dragged Jenna to Courtney's room where she forced Jenna to knock on the door. No one knew that Circe had hurried into the room when Lisa and Jenna were in the hall. Courtney opened the door, and while threatening them with a knife, Lisa pulled Jenna inside. Angie arrived before the door could be locked again.

Despite their preparation and training, everything that could have gone wrong did, but the Roseland family still had a few tricks up their sleeves and used them to their advantage.

On the way to Courtney's room, Ellie had spotted Tom on the floor of the upstairs hallway. She knelt beside him and lay her hands on the man as she had with Rufus. In moments, she knew Tom's head injury had been healed. Then she made her way to Courtney's room and waited in the hall for Mr. Finch and Euclid to join her. Working together, they were finally able to take Lisa down.

By the time their statements had been taken and people had returned from the hospital, the sun was rising on Courtney and Rufus' wedding day.

"Are you sure you don't want to postpone?" Angie had asked them.

"There's no way we're postponing," Rufus announced as he took Courtney's hand. "I'm marrying the love of my life even if I have to crawl down that aisle."

Courtney hugged him. "I wouldn't want it any other way."

With a cast on her arm, Jenna said, "I got this broken arm trying to protect my family so Courtney and Rufus could marry today. We triumphed over adversity, and we're going to have a big beautiful celebration because we're all still here."

"A little worse for wear, but still here." Mr. Finch's face was full of joy.

After eating breakfast, Courtney, Rufus, and his mother sat outside by the fire pit, where she explained to them that she'd always had fire power, but she didn't know how to handle it so pushed the ability down and only used it on occasion. When Rufus was little, Susan sensed he had inherited her skill, but she never talked with him about it. She had no idea he'd found it while living in Sweet Cove and was overjoyed to hear he'd been able to use it for good. Susan didn't know if her ancestors had the skill because no one ever spoke of it. When she met the Roselands, she sensed they had some powers and was delighted to know Rufus was marrying into such a family.

"I don't think today could be any more wonderful," Susan told Courtney and Rufus as she shared a long, heartfelt hug with them.

It was early evening when the guests began to gather in the gardens for the wedding, and as the sun headed to the horizon, it cast its warm, beautiful light over the yard full of flowers.

A light ocean breeze drifted through the open

windows, carrying the scent of roses and gardenias from the flower gardens surrounding the Victorian mansion. The living room was simply but beautifully decorated for Courtney and Rufus' special day. A garland of baby's breath and roses adorned the fireplace mantle. Candles flickered on the end tables, filling the room with a warm, romantic glow.

Before changing into their gowns and suits, the Roseland family gathered in the living room before the ceremony.

Angie turned to Courtney and Rufus with a grin. "We have a surprise for you two," she said, pointing to a small box on the living room table. "The family had these made for you."

Rufus leaned in as Courtney opened the box to reveal two matching gold bracelets. Engraved on each one was the date of their wedding, along with a special message: "Now and Forever."

"Oh my gosh, they're beautiful," Courtney exclaimed, tears welling up in her eyes as she turned to Rufus. "It's what you said to me when we were on the boat for dinner with the family; you said you'd be by my side now and forever."

"How did you know what I said to Courtney?" he asked the family members.

"We didn't know," Mr. Finch told them and then winked. "I guess it's a coincidence."

Rufus took a bracelet from Courtney's hand and fastened it around her wrist, and then she did the same for him.

"Thank you so much. This means the world to us," Rufus said, his voice filled with emotion. "To quote Mr. Finch, my life began when I met this family. How I love you all."

In just a short while, the loving couple would exchange their vows under the white tent set up on the sweeping back lawn. Rows of white folding chairs faced an archway entwined with roses, daisies, and greenery. At the end of the aisle, Chief Martin waited to officiate the ceremony with Circe, standing on his right wearing a pink ribbon, and Euclid with a bowtie around his neck standing on the other side. Soft music from acoustic guitars floated on the air.

Courtney looked radiant in her lace wedding dress, clutching her bouquet of blush and cream-colored roses. Rufus stood tall and handsome in his navy blue suit, a smile lighting up his face. Their family and closest friends gathered around them, joy and excitement sparkling in everyone's eyes.

"It's time," Angie said, giving Courtney a careful hug. "I'm so happy for you both."

The guests took their seats facing the flower-adorned arch. Rufus walked his mother and father down the aisle, then took his place under the arbor. Josh, Tom, and Jack were next to walk the aisle to the front of the gathering, and after them came little Libby and Gigi, carefully tossing rose petals along the white runner. Ellie, wearing the glowing moonstone necklace, Jenna, and Angie came next, their faces beaming with joy for their sister.

The music changed to the traditional wedding march as Mr. Finch proudly escorted the radiant bride down the aisle. Rufus watched with tears in his eyes, scarcely able to believe this magical moment had finally arrived. Chief Martin, dressed in his formal police uniform, smiled as Courtney and Mr. Finch took their places under the archway.

"Family and friends, we are gathered here today to celebrate the love, strength, and devotion between Courtney and Rufus," Chief Martin began. His deep voice carried clearly in the tranquil, sunny garden. "Their love has grown and flourished since the moment they first met by chance here in Sweet Cove."

The chief spoke eloquently about the couple's

journey, overcoming hardships and finding strength in their bond, and then it was time for the vows.

Rufus took Courtney's hand, his eyes never leaving her glowing face.

"Courtney, from the first time I saw you, I knew you were my soulmate, the missing piece of my heart. Our relationship hasn't always been easy, but we've only grown closer. I vow to stand by your side in joy and hardship, to make you laugh when times are tough, and to nurture our love so it grows stronger with each passing day. I will love and cherish you now and forever."

Tears slipped down Courtney's cheeks as she recited her own heartfelt vows. "Rufus, you are my best friend, my confidant, my home. Your unwavering love and strength have seen me through dark times and lifted me up. I vow to be your partner, your ally, your sanctuary as we walk through life hand in hand. In laughter and tears, through adventures and quiet moments, I will love you now and always."

With a wide smile, Chief Martin pronounced them husband and wife.

As they shared their first kiss as husband and wife, a roar of applause went up from the delighted guests. Magill stepped forward, her flowing silk dress catching the light, and raised her hands over the couple's heads.

"May you be blessed with a long life together overflowing with love, joy, and fulfillment," she intoned, closing her eyes. "May you use your many skills and talents for good and for joy. Go in love to share your gifts. Make the world a better place because you are in it together."

A faint shimmering glow seemed to surround Rufus and Courtney for a moment before gently fading away.

Laughing, the newlyweds led the guests to the wide back patio and pergola where champagne glasses waited on silver trays. The sparkling wine flowed as everyone congratulated the couple, applauded the beautiful ceremony, and snapped countless pictures. Strings of lights twinkled in the trees as the sun began to set behind the Victorian home.

Soon it was time to board the shuttle buses that would carry the guests down to the harbor, where Josh's luxurious yacht waited. The sleek white boat bobbed gently in its slip, decorated with flowers and ribbons just for the special occasion.

Courtney and Rufus lingered behind, walking arm in arm through the rose garden while a photographer captured romantic images of the newly married couple. Their joy was shining brightly, lighting up the deepening twilight. This perfect day was just the beginning of a new life together, full of love and family.

When Courtney and Rufus arrived at the dock, Euclid and Circe proudly led the newly-married couple up the gangplank to the yacht.

The sleek white yacht gently rocked on the sparkling water as the happy couple arrived to cheers and applause from their delighted guests waiting on the spacious deck.

Potted palms and floral arrangements added bright pops of color, and strings of twinkling lights were woven through the railings. At the front of the boat, musicians played upbeat music, welcoming everyone aboard for the celebration.

The couple made their way around the deck, stopping to chat and laugh with their friends and family. Waiters in crisp white shirts circulated with trays of champagne, wine, and appetizers. The mood was joyful and celebratory.

"I'm so happy for you both," Angie said, hugging her sister and her brother-in-law.

"We're all thrilled for you," Ellie added, her arm around Jack.

Rufus grinned and squeezed Courtney's hand. "We're the luckiest people in the world."

Soon it was time to move inside the yacht's elegant dining room for dinner. The long table was draped with a white linen cloth and set with china, crystal, and flickering candles. Garlands of flowers decorated the walls, and a huge bouquet served as the table centerpiece.

More acoustic guitar music played softly as the guests took their seats. Waiters appeared with the first course of lobster bisque, followed by salads of baby greens and roasted vegetables. The main course was a duo of filet mignon and seared salmon with lemony risotto and asparagus.

Laughter and happy conversation flowed around the table as everyone enjoyed the meal. Mr. Finch gave a touching toast to the newlyweds, wishing them a long lifetime of joy and togetherness. He recalled how fortunate they were to have found one another.

"To Courtney and Rufus," he concluded, raising his glass, and everyone echoed the sentiment before taking sips of champagne.

When the dessert course arrived - a gorgeous three-tiered cake with flavors of red velvet and white chocolate - Courtney turned to Angie with a smile.

"This cake is incredible, Angie. Thank you so much."

Angie beamed, pleased that her baking talents had helped make the day special. She smiled. "Anything for my little sister."

After dinner, the guests returned to the flower-adorned deck to dance under the stars. The band played lively tunes as everyone crowded the dance floor. Courtney and Rufus glowed with joy as they swayed in one another's arms.

Courtney leaned in close so Rufus could hear her over the music. "I feel my mom and Nana are here with us. I feel them all around me. I could sense they were with us during the attack last night. I was scared when Lisa had me in a stranglehold, but deep down, I had the feeling I was going to be all right."

Rufus nodded, holding her tighter. "I'm sure their spirits are watching over us. This is a celebration of love - that's what they would want for us."

A few minutes later, Jenna hurried over to her sisters with a big smile and a few tears in her eyes. "I saw Barri's ghost. She looked happy. I thanked her for her message to keep both of you safe. When Barri disappeared, Mom and Nana materialized. They were so happy. I know they're thrilled about your marriage. They put their hands over their hearts and slowly sparkled away."

Ellie came over and they told her about the ghosts, and they all got teary-eyed, sharing a warm group hug.

As the evening wound down, the guests gradually departed into waiting taxis on the dock. Heartfelt hugs and congratulations were exchanged as everyone said their goodbyes. Soon it was just the Roseland family lingering on the softly rocking yacht.

When they settled into cushy chairs out on the moonlit deck, Josh and Tom passed around mugs of hot coffee laced with Bailey's while Euclid and Circe curled up nearby.

"I'm a little wistful," Angie remarked. "Courtney is the last of us to get married. We won't have any other weddings to put on."

"Well," Mr. Finch said, "Gigi and Libby will grow up and they will most likely get married someday, and I intend to be there for those two marvelous days."

Euclid and Circe both trilled and meowed.

"I think the cats plan on being at their weddings, too." Angie laughed.

"We wouldn't have it any other way," Ellie smiled, stroking Circe's soft fur.

Under the sparkling stars, Courtney snuggled closer to Rufus with a contented sigh. "I know we'll all be together always, whether in spirit or in the flesh. We're in each other's hearts ... now and forever."

THANK YOU FOR READING! RECIPES BELOW!

Books by J.A. WHITING can be found here:
amazon.com/author/jawhiting

To hear about new books and book sales, please sign up for my mailing list at:
jawhiting.com

Your email will never be sold, shared, or spammed.

If you enjoyed the book, please consider leaving a review. A few words are all that's needed. It would be very much appreciated.

BOOKS BY J. A. WHITING

SWEET COVE PARANORMAL COZY MYSTERIES

LIN COFFIN PARANORMAL COZY MYSTERIES

CLAIRE ROLLINS PARANORMAL COZY MYSTERIES

MURDER POSSE PARANORMAL COZY MYSTERIES

PAXTON PARK PARANORMAL COZY MYSTERIES

ELLA DANIELS WITCH COZY MYSTERIES

SEEING COLORS PARANORMAL COZY MYSTERIES

OLIVIA MILLER MYSTERIES (not cozy)

SWEET ROMANCES by JENA WINTER

COZY BOX SETS

BOOKS BY J.A. WHITING & NELL MCCARTHY

HOPE HERRING PARANORMAL COZY MYSTERIES

TIPPERARY CARRIAGE COMPANY COZY MYSTERIES

BOOKS BY J.A. WHITING & ARIEL SLICK

GOOD HARBOR WITCHES PARANORMAL COZY
MYSTERIES

BOOKS BY J.A. WHITING & AMANDA DIAMOND

PEACHTREE POINT COZY MYSTERIES

DIGGING UP SECRETS PARANORMAL COZY MYSTERIES

BOOKS BY J.A. WHITING & MAY STENMARK

MAGICAL SLEUTH PARANORMAL WOMEN'S FICTION COZY MYSTERIES

HALF MOON PARANORMAL MYSTERIES

VISIT US

jawhiting.com

bookbub.com/authors/j-a-whiting

amazon.com/author/jawhiting

facebook.com/jawhitingauthor

bingebooks.com/author/ja-whiting

SOME RECIPES FROM THE SWEET COVE SERIES

Recipes

SOME RECIPES FROM THE SWEET COVE SERIES

Recipes

ENGLISH SCONES

INGREDIENTS

2 cups cake flour

½ teaspoon salt

2 teaspoons baking powder

3 Tablespoons sugar

5-6 Tablespoons cold butter, cut into pieces

1 large egg

¾ cup heavy cream (can use fat free milk, fat free half and half, almond milk, etc)

DIRECTIONS

Heat oven to 450°F (or if using convection, 425°F.)

Place flour, salt, baking powder, and 2 Tablespoons sugar into food processor; pulse until the mixture looks like cornmeal.

Add the egg and just enough cream to make slightly sticky dough.

Turn dough onto lightly floured surface; Knead.

Press the dough into a ¾ inch round.

Use a 2 inch glass or biscuit cutter to make 2 inch rounds.

Reshape leftover dough into another round and cut again.

Place the rounds on a baking sheet covered with parchment paper.

Brush the tops of the scones with a little cream and sprinkle each with a tiny amount of sugar.

Bake for about 10 minutes or until the scones are light golden brown.

Serve with jam, berries, or whipped cream.

Makes 8-10 scones.

FRENCH TOAST BAKE

INGREDIENTS

1 loaf day old French bread (can also use challah or sour dough) (about 8-10 cups)

2 cups milk

7 large eggs

½ cup packed brown sugar

¾ teaspoon cinnamon

Pinch of salt

INGREDIENTS FOR THE TOPPING

½ cup salted butter, cubed

½ cup all-purpose flour

⅓ cup packed brown sugar

1 cup berries (can use frozen or fresh)

DIRECTIONS

Grease 9 x 13 casserole dish.

Cut the bread into cubes and layer in the pan (should have two layers).

Beat milk, eggs, brown sugar, cinnamon, and salt in a medium size bowl.

Pour the mixture evenly over the bread. Be sure to cover all the pieces.

Cover with foil and refrigerate overnight (or at least 4 hours).

DIRECTIONS FOR THE TOPPING

In a medium sized bowl, mix together butter, flour, and brown sugar with two knives, a pastry cutter, or your hands.

DIRECTIONS FOR BAKING

Preheat oven to 350°F.

Spread the crumb topping over the bread mixture.

Place berries over the top.

Bake uncovered for 50-60 minutes, or until the top is lightly browned and the center is cooked through.

*Serve with maple syrup, fresh berries, powdered sugar, and/or whipped cream.

SHORTBREAD COOKIES

INGREDIENTS

10 Tablespoons unsalted butter, room temperature

½ cup confectioner's sugar

½ teaspoon pure vanilla extract

1½ cups all-purpose flour

½ teaspoon kosher salt (may be omitted)

DIRECTIONS

Beat butter and vanilla until creamed.

Mix in confectioner's sugar and salt until combined.

Scrape down the bowl; Add the flour; Beat on low until combined.

Shape the dough into a rectangular shape; Wrap in plastic wrap, and chill 1 – 1 ½ hours.

Preheat the oven to 350°F.

Use a sharp knife to cut into ½ inch thick slices.

Place slices, an inch apart, on a parchment-lined baking sheet.

Use a fork or a skewer to indent a pattern onto the cookie tops.

Bake for about 10 minutes; rotate the baking sheet halfway through the baking.

Transfer to wire rack to cool.

TACO CASSEROLE

INGREDIENTS

1 pound ground beef or vegetarian meat substitute

½ yellow onion, chopped

2 Tablespoons taco seasoning

1 cup salsa

¼ cup water

1 15-ounce can black beans, drained and rinsed

1½ cups frozen corn

1½ cups cheese blend

3 cups tortilla chips

DIRECTIONS

Preheat oven to 375°F.

Lightly coat a baking dish with cooking spray.

Cook beef and chopped onion in a large skillet over medium-high heat; Drain excess grease.

Reduce heat to low, add taco seasoning, salsa, water, black beans, and corn. Stir to combine and cook until warm through.

Pour mixture in prepared pan. Sprinkle with cheese.

Lightly crush tortilla chips and spread evenly over the top.

Bake for 15-20 minutes, until cheese is melted.

Enjoy!

Made in United States
North Haven, CT
09 May 2024

52322365R00189